Diving on the Anchor

Bridget Arregger

Copyright © Bridget Arregger 2024

All Rights Reserved

No part of this publication may be reproduced, distributed, or transmitted in any form or by any means, including photocopying, recording, or other electronic or mechanical methods, without the author's prior written permission, except in the case of brief quotations embodied in critical reviews and certain other non-commercial uses permitted by copyright law. For permission requests, please get in touch with the author.

Contents

Dedication	i
Acknowledgements	ii
About the Author	iii
Oh Good it's Daylight!	1
Coffee, Toast and Three Paracetamol	3
Out of Curiosity	5
Nine o'clock on a Sunday Morning	11
Trompeta, Hello and Farewell	15
Los Roches	20
Tigrilla Squid	27
Diving on the Anchor	29
Three Trees and Somebody Tief de Gas	33
Dartington Hall – an Imagined Visit	35
Writing is . . .	37
You're a Natural Poet	38
When I am busily writing	38
Jersey Saltram	39
On the Spectrum	41
Skipping	45
Creative Acrostic	48
Bicycle Surprise	49
Morgan	52
Garden Fairies	54
My Garden in Autumn	57
From Cotswolds to East Midlands	59
God knows	62
Beehives and Biohazards	66
Lottery	72
Fetch!	73
Getaway	75
Blue Willow Trigger	78
The Sky's the Limit	79
How I Met John	83
Your Beard	86
The Birds	89
Clothes Maketh Women	92
Alter-ego	98
Her Decision	101
Moving on	103
March or Dance? The Changing Use of Rhythm in Poetry	104
What's in Your Pockets?	105
Serendipity	107
Grief and Laughter	109
One Year Older	111
Great Aunt Zilla	113
Haunted	116
My Name is Sandra	117
VHF Possibilities	121

Dedication

To my parents

Acknowledgements

I extend my heartfelt thanks to Somewhere Else Writers, Towcester Writers, and Daventry U3A Creative Writing Group for their attentive ears, constructive criticism, and laughter in all the right places.

Anthologies, where stories have been included,
- "Oh Good It's Daylight" first appeared in Autumn 2020 in the Towcester Town Crier and later in 2023 in "Coffee Break Companion," the second anthology of the Towcester Writers' Group.
- "VHF Possibilities" was first printed in October 1999 in the Boca, Trinidad & Tobago's Waterfront Newspaper, and in 2022, it found its place in "Off The Wall," the second anthology of the Somewhere Else Writers, accompanied by an audio link.
- "Out of Curiosity" made its debut in 2019 within the pages of "Pick 'n Mix," the first anthology of the Towcester Writers' Group. Later, in 2022, it was also featured in "Off The Wall," the second anthology of the Somewhere Else Writers, along with an audio link.
- "Moving On," "On the Spectrum," and "The Sky's the Limit" all came to life in 2023 within the pages of "Coffee Break Companion," the Towcester Writers' Group's second anthology.

Thank you for your ongoing support and for joining me on this literary adventure.
Warm regards,
Bridget

About the Author

Bridget Arregger, formerly known as Adams, is a seasoned writer with a rich history in academia and a passion for storytelling. During her career, she authored three textbooks and contributed various articles to teaching journals. Upon retiring, Bridget reignited her lifelong enthusiasm for crafting narratives, finding joy in the creative process of blending fact with fiction.

Her literary journey has seen her short stories and poems featured in local magazines and anthologies, earning recognition in competitions and being broadcast on local radio. Bridget's preferred genre is speculative fiction, where she delves into the realms of science fiction, fantasy, and dreams. Drawing from her experiences as an educator and her adventures sailing the Caribbean with her husband, she weaves elements of autobiography into her tales.

Bridget is an active member of the literary community, leading the editorial team of her village newsletter and serving as a founding member of Somewhere Else Writers in Cirencester. Currently, she is engaged with Towcester Writers and the U3A creative writing group in Daventry, further honing her craft alongside fellow enthusiasts.

Other books by Bridget

Fiction

Climbing the Mast: a collection of short stories and poems, 2015.

Switching, Switching: a sci-fi adventure, 2018

Non-fiction (in the former name of Adams),

The Psychology Companion. Adams, B. (2009) Basingstoke: Palgrave Macmillan

Psychology for Health Care: Key Terms and Concepts. Adams B. & Bromley B. (1998) Basingstoke: Macmillan

ABC of Communication Studies, 2nd edn Gill D. & Adams B. (1998). London: Nelson.

Outside of her literary pursuits, Bridget finds fulfilment in family life, cherishing her role as mother to two sons and grandmother to four teenagers.

For more insights into Bridget's work and interests, visit her website: https://www.bridgetarregger.uk.

Oh Good it's Daylight!

Doggy tails:

5 a.m. Oh good, it's daylight. I think I'll get up and potter around. Have a good stretch. Don't need a pee but I think I'll go out in the garden. I scratch at the garden door. Ah, the door won't open. I'll growl at it; that sometimes works. No, it won't work. Few good barks. No, nothing. She's upstairs; she can't hear me. I think I'll howl. That usually makes the door open.

Come on, Loki, time for a good howl, better when it's both of us. Ah yes, bed creaking. She's coming downstairs. Uh oh! That's the grumpy stomp. That doesn't usually mean that the door will open. I'd better start wagging my tail now. That usually helps. Finish the howling and be all innocent when she comes in. Here she comes. I'll prance about on my hind legs. Mustn't touch her; she won't like that, and she'll use the command "Off!" I do my best dance without touching. She doesn't take any notice, but I know she likes it. Uh oh! Here comes the cross voice: "Go to bed!" Then something else I don't understand but sounds familiar.

Then again, "Go to bed!". OK, OK, tail between my legs now. Nose into bed or try to; but Loki is over in my bed now in my warm patch. Stand and Wait. Put on my pathetic, helpless posture. She bends down and feels that Loki is inside my blanket. She lifts the other blanket so I can climb into Loki's bed. I go over and sniff.

Stinks of him. I walk away. Uh oh! Very cross voice, "Arianna! Go to bed, now!" OK, OK, I'm going. I slide under the stinky blanket. I shut my eyes.

I hear the kitchen door closing. Grumpy footsteps going upstairs. I hear the bed creak. If I bark, she'll come back down. I'd like her to come back. But I don't like the cross voice. I'm sleepy now. I keep my eyes closed.

8 a.m. Oh good, it's daylight. I think I'll get up and potter around. Have a good stretch. I don't need a pee, but there's a pigeon on the fence. The garden door won't open. Loki is standing by the door, waiting. OK, I'll wait with him. I hear water splashing upstairs. She'll come down soon.

Here she is. Smiley face. I do my best dance on my hind legs without touching. She pats my head. "Hello doggies". Happy voice. I make a soft, friendly hello growl. I scratch at the door. She taps me on the nose and then uses a command, "Wait!" So I wait. Loki is sitting down. OK, I can sit too. That usually works. The door opens, and I rush out to say hello to the pigeons, and the voles and the moles, and the neighbours and the trains and the flowers, and everybody and …. Uh oh! Cross voice "No barking!" OK, OK. Hello world!

Coffee, Toast and Three Paracetamol

Detective Inspector Derek Cotman sniffed the dregs of coffee, wrinkling his nose at the faint trace of almond. He eyed the half-eaten toast and empty packets of paracetamol with evident distaste. Three tablets lay scattered on the carpet. The body was slumped over the table, a blank sheet of paper trapped under one hand, a pencil gripped tightly in the other.

Who was she? Why did she want to die? What drove her to this?

All the hallmarks of suicide and yet ... and yet DI Cotman knew from experience that this could be the accurately staged cover for the perfect murder, and there was that suspicious tang of almond suggestive of cyanide poisoning.

Careful questioning of the neighbours revealed that she was, or had been, Sylvia Smith, recently separated from her husband. More careful questioning led to a neighbour reporting seeing a man sporting a fashionable beard and an obvious beer belly, who had been a regular visitor, entering the apartment the day before. DI Cotman stroked his clean-shaven chin and sucked in his flat stomach with pride. He gave out a small grunt of contempt. DS Angela Murphy was looking puzzled.

'Sir,' she enquired, 'why would such a fit young woman, who evidently worked out regularly, want to date someone who did not share that obsession?'

'Perhaps he had other attributes,' DI Cotman replied with a leer. He chose to interpret her expression of disgust in a way that was flattering to his ego. She moved away before he could pat her shoulder.

They left the building in silence, each preoccupied with their thoughts.

DI Cotman hummed to himself as he entered the station. The postmortem would reveal nothing untoward: merely liver failure from repeated overdoses of paracetamol over the past few weeks and Amaretto in the coffee. Cyanide poisoning would be ruled out. The fat bearded man would not be found. The case would be closed. Another life wasted. Another satisfactory outcome.

He scratched absent-mindedly at his jaw, then stared blankly for a moment at the sticky scrap of latex glue that was caught under his fingernail. He was getting careless. That wouldn't do.

Creative Writing Group prompt: Coffee, toast and three paracetamol.

Out of Curiosity

Widely known as a local artist and with something of a reputation as a restorer, I have been given the task of cleaning some paintings in a pub. I take the first one home.

It's a big painting - two metres by a metre-and-a-half. It depicts a Victorian cow with river, hills and mountains in the background, and with grasses and ripe wheat in the foreground. It is a curious mixture of typical Victorian and something indefinably *not* Victorian.

The paint is darkened after a few years in the pub when smoking was allowed. It is surprising how dirty paintings become from smoke and beer. The back of the canvas is discoloured and stained. It looks older than the ornate but cheap gilt frame that is stamped 'made in Taiwan'.

It is not valuable - not in the category of potboiler, but not authentic, and with poor brushstrokes. It is an amateurish attempt. It will not matter if I damage it. I could paint them a new and better one.

I remove the canvas from the frame and begin the initial stages of washing with warm water with a touch of ammonia to remove the superficial dirt, drying it with a soft cloth to prevent the water from seeping into the canvas.

Then, to remove the varnish. A scribbled note on the back of the frame tells me that, unlike older paintings, this has been finished with modern polymer removable varnish, so this is a simple job of wiping with a slightly stronger solution of ammonia, section by section so that the canvas does not become saturated. I open all the windows and endure the choking smell.

I stand back. The painting is now bright and light and looks freshly painted. Probably, that is all that is needed. I give it a second wiping with clean water and put it aside in sunlight to dry thoroughly and brighten still further, while I buy some new dammar varnish. This will give a slightly less glossy finish and sit better on the oil paint.

I flip the canvas over to deal with the back, carefully cleaning out the trapped dust. No cigarette butts or drawing pins. Or coins. But as I remove the last wedge, I see a tiny corner of paper peeping out from under the canvas. I fetch tweezers and gently draw the paper out. It is a brief love letter on computer printer paper, saying,

'My love, I know how you adore cows. This young virginal heifer looks as if she has a secret to tell - she is soulful and curious about you. Are you curious about her?' L.V.

I go back to the painting and notice there appears to be a red underpainting. Some of the red is revealed with each scratch and twist of a pointed stick that has been used to depict the stems of

Out of Curiosity

wheat. This is a technique I love but I think of it as being recently introduced, more recent than Victorian. Not merely the varnish and frame are new.

I *Googled* 'Victorian Cow Paintings' and found a poster for sale of *The Craven Heifer* from a painting and engraving by *Fryer* and *Whessell* in 1811. The cow is almost identical, but the background is significantly different. My curiosity is now piqued; I buy a copy of the poster and lay them side by side. The poster is twenty inches by sixteen, about a quarter of the size of the canvas, and designed to fit standard frames.

The pub painting is not skilfully painted. Nice technique with the red underpainting, though. *That* does not appear in the poster. The scratching indicates some knowledge and skill on the part of the painter. Most likely, he used the end of his paintbrush. As someone has pointed out, you may use the hard point and the brush - you have paid for both ends.

I pick away at the paint in the lower left corner, gradually revealing the dark green plant of the poster version under the modern irises. I also find the hidden folly further up on the left. Was the artist worried about copyright even for a common painting like this? Or couldn't paint competently? But why cover the original? It's popular and readily available as a poster. Why conceal the earlier one? Vanity perhaps. Wanting to pass off the painting as his own. Or her own. I examine the signature. Initials only. *L.V.* Is that real? A code?

A joke? Love? Lover? Elvie? Perhaps this modern artist is the writer of the love letter. Perhaps not. No clue as to the identity or date, but recent, not Victorian. Is someone practising painting? Using someone else's painting as a base?

As I take off more paint, I find it is a paper poster underneath. It has been blown up in sections from the original size, pasted on and painted over. Curiouser and curiouser. What is this amateur thinking of? Saving money? Picked up an old canvas in a junk shop? Pasted the print over it and painted over to make it their own? Wanting to impress the lover?

I stand back. There appears to be a pattern to the underpainting, with variations in the red occurring in straight lines.

I pick away at the straight lines. Disappointingly, they are merely the joins in the sections of the enlarged poster. I had half expected another letter, cunningly hidden in the thick paint. I stand back and survey the mess I have made of the cow. No going back now. If the pub owners want the cow, I shall have to honour my foolish boast and paint them one. What have I got to lose? Wild optimism, or meddlesomeness, prompts me to continue digging.

I'm not sure whether I am astonished or vindicated when, as I remove some of the paper, I find another layer of paint.

Out of Curiosity

This is getting serious. I begin to photograph repeatedly as I start to remove the poster carefully, miniscule fragment by miniscule fragment, with a scalpel.

Parts of a further painting are gradually uncovered. It is an ugly scene of rape and hacking with swords and spears, with devils and monsters. No wonder our modern lover covered it over. I dread what I will find. I can't go on. I put it aside in horror.

That night, I dream of devils and angels. I wake with a strange sense of *déjà vu*. Of dread and despair mixed with hope and lightness. The painting is obscurely familiar, so I have a closer look and *Google* 'devil paintings'. I remove more of the poster and expose a poorly executed copy of a painting by Pieter Bruegel the Elder - *The Fall of the Rebel Angels* of 1562. There are some noticeable differences so this may be an earlier attempt by Breugel or, more likely, poor artisanry by the copier. As I lightly clean this of sticky paste and other grime and dirt, my cloth tells my fingertips there are more straight lines. Gently, I pick at the next layer of paint. This time, I do find a letter buried in the pigment. This earlier artist has painted thickly over Breugel's canvas to match the original as competently as possible and thus conceal the letter.

However, that is not quite the case. The fine velour document tells of the dissolution of the monasteries during the reign of Henry VIII in the 1540s.

Bridget Arregger

Perhaps a monk, not a skilled painter, but a clever one, has hidden not only the letter but copied over something he wanted to protect from the pillage of the monasteries by the king.

With the help of restorers more expert than me, we discover a rare, old, beautiful and extremely valuable painting - an early version of the striking and unusual *Virgin of the Rocks* by Leonardo da Vinci from about 1490.

The faces of the Virgin and child are lit by sunshine and engender hope, in contrast to the dark, sombre rocks of the surroundings.

Prompt: theme of Pandora's box, or hope arising out of chaos and evil.

Nine o'clock on a Sunday Morning

Love in the Time of Covid: Susie

At nine o'clock on a Sunday morning, after a first trimester of anxiety and ensuing months of ever-increasing joy, Susie and Timothy Ellis were making love cautiously and delicately. After six years of wanting to give Ben a baby brother or sister, they were soon to give him both. The huge mound of Susie's belly was glistening and slippery with baby oil.

'Darling, that is so good – I didn't expect to enjoy this so late on.'

'And you haven't lost your figure – you are leaner apart from the bump. I'm not the only one who thinks so, from what you were telling me.'

'Those builders? That was funny – you should have seen their faces.'

'It's the black trousers that do it.'

'You think so? They're ordinary trousers.'

'It's not an ordinary bum, and you have developed a delightful wiggle with all that weight up front.'

'Have I? It's true I get more comments now – from behind. And when they came level, all those men in the pick-up truck, their jaws dropped, and then they started clapping – I don't know which they saw first, the belly or the dog collar.'

'The . . . Good god! Pardon me, God. What on earth was that noise downstairs?'

'Ooh, intruders! Time to don your cloak and knickers.'

'Sounded more like Father Christmas coming down the chimney. Another bird, I bet. The day anyone thinks there is anything worth pinching from the curates' house will be the day to exchange our cassocks for blue and red cloaks. Hang on, no need for both of us to go.'

Timothy, without bothering to 'don' anything, sauntered down the bare wooden stairs and investigated the fireplace in the living room. He could hear frantic rustling, and he stood to one side as he pulled the gas fire out of the way and opened up the chimney. A startled starling, dazed but not slow to see the way out, hopped past him and out onto the carpet, leaving a small trail of soot. Timothy opened the French windows, left the bird to find its way out of the house and went back up to his wife.

'Time we fixed something over the chimney pot. That's the third, or is it the fourth since we moved in? Ah, excuse me, I'm

Nine o'clock on a Sunday Morning

going to sneeze; it must be the soot. Have we had the chimney swept? Now, where were we?'

'Just there, thank you.'

'Here? Like this? Good? And you were telling me about the workers ...'

'Yes, one of them insisted on asking me which church, and when I told him, he said he'd be there today – asked me the time and everything. I must look out for him. I know it's old-fashioned to wear the clerical collar, and we're certainly not obliged to, before being ordained, but I like it. It gives me a sense of identity. Do you think God would approve of me recruiting new members in this way?'

'I'm sure God would heartily approve, my angel. He knew what he was doing when he made us. I dare say he was half hoping Adam *would* eat the fruit; even if Adam was such a wimp, he wouldn't dare until Eve picked some and then blamed her. What a jerk! Bit of all right, old Eve – feisty lady. If there are any planets where the equivalent of A and E are still respectfully avoiding the tree, they must be hellishly dull. There's not much point in God hanging around. As for being old-fashioned, getting wolf whistles is decidedly retro.'

'They didn't actually whistle...'

'Now, how're we doing, my feisty lady?'

'Very nicely, thank you. This is so-o-o good; you know.'

'Do you think they're enjoying this too?' Timothy asked. 'I can feel one of them kicking against my hands.'

'I'm sure they are enjoying the massage. Who wouldn't?'

'Do you think it will be all right to make you come?'

'I hope so; it's about the last chance I'll have for your undivided attention for . . . years! We're lucky to have this weekend to ourselves now that Ben is old enough to go on sleepovers. It's not as if either of us has parents able and willing to babysit. And twins? We can't inflict that on many people! It'll be quite gentle, not like contractions. Anyhow, it won't matter if we set off the real thing. One of them, and I'll place no bets on whether it's the boy or the girl, butts my pelvis like a kid, the baby goat sort. It's a couple of weeks to go, and they feel ready to come now.'

'And you, Susie, my love, are you ready to come now?'

'Yes, please, yes, exactly there . . .'

'Oh my god, the church bells. Is that the time?'

'Must we go?'

'I think we might be missed.'

Trompeta, Hello and Farewell

Trompeta Sailing Diaries: Friday 25 July 1997

John has sailed his yacht, Trompeta, to Margarita and is ready for me to arrive. I have taken a year's unpaid leave and will be a kept woman for the duration. We plan to explore many of the islands of the Caribbean together. I had two weeks of initiation into sailing with John in Spain last summer and learned a few knots. My adventure is about to begin. Our friends, Simon and Janice, who have sailed with John before, are travelling with me, and we plan to cruise around Los Roches, a group of islands off the coast of Venezuela, for their holiday.

Simon, Janice and I leave home before 05:00 for H/R 06:00 and depart a couple of hours later. We arrive in Margarita via Madrid and Caracas on time at 19:40 in the evening. The plane from Caracas to Margarita is a small local prop, shaky and of questionable safety . . . and everyone cheers as we land.

John will meet us at the airport with taxi. It is dark. It is hot. All of us are hot and tired but it's not too bad as the journey had been straightforward with enough time for both changes.

Short taxi ride and then we clamber onboard. It feels good to be here if smelly. Hello again, Trompeta.

On Saturday, Janice and Simon rush off at 9:00 for the bus to Provideria to buy essentials for the weekend. We are expecting two more friends, Ruth and Derek, to contact us at some point. By coincidence, they are visiting Margarita this week and will be staying in one of the big hotels at the beach.

I help John drain water out of the diesel. This arose from mistaking Water Baby for Diesel Man. In Margarita, there is no fuel dock in the harbour so small quaintly-named barges bring water and fuel out to the boats. For a small charge. (Quite a large charge, having a captive consumer group with specific needs.)

The day before, John had radioed for fuel and at about the time he was expecting it, a barge hailed him with tank and hoses; he said go ahead and opened the fuel inlet on the deck. As they started to fuel up, he said disparagingly,

'That looks like water.'

'It _is_ water,' the guy said.

Quick stop!!

It is a laborious job draining the tank.

We have a late lunch on Janice and Simon's triumphant return with plenty of food and drink. We all rest, desperately aware of the need for a siesta. It gets dark early, rapidly, in the tropics, and as the afternoon threatens to leave us, we take the dinghy ashore and go to the Vemasca office to arrange for them to check us in with the port authorities.

Janice and I have a quick swim around the boat before starting supper. Told later it is not advisable to swim in the marina as all the yachts void their toilets into the bay. There are no health and safety restrictions here.

When supper is nearly ready, Ruth and Derek radio. They have arrived at the bar on the beach. There follows a bizarre conversation as I try to sort out about meeting them ashore without ruining our supper. John had answered Derek's call (Derek is a pilot and accustomed to the radio), then changed channels and handed me over to Ruth. My first time using the VHF, with no introduction. Ruth is also new to it.

I assume it is like a telephone and expensive, charged by the minute or second. I manage to press the button to speak and let go again to listen, but I do not know more than that. We have long pauses while I consult the others about when to go ashore, before or after supper. Ruth and I were hesitant and slow. I worry about the bill mounting up and others queuing to use the phone/radio.

To add to the general delay and confusion, John announces that we cannot go ashore as we are out of petrol for the outboard as we had run out earlier on our trip to Vemasca. Moreover, to make life complicated, he reminded me the safety pin had sheared when the propeller scraped the bottom when we left the dock. I wasn't sure what that entailed, but John had to row us back. He did not want to row again today, and in any case, we could not buy fuel at this time of night, and he certainly wasn't rowing both ways. There is a noticeable lack of volunteering from his various crew members. An inflatable rubber dinghy with a floppy bottom is a bugger to row. Is there any way in which Ruth and Derek could come out to the boat or should we wait until tomorrow when someone could row ashore and buy some fuel? I try to relay all this to Ruth amidst much inaccurate key pressing. Then, an accented voice interrupts us.

'Trompeta, Farewell.'

Huh?

'No,' I cry, 'we haven't finished.' I think it must be the telephone exchange, not English-speaking, saying our time was up. 'No, not farewell,' I cry, 'we need longer, more time, please.'

I can't speak Spanish. I cannot begin to explain. Frantic, I signal to John. This time, he hears clearly.

'Trompeta, Trompeta, Farewell.'

'What's up,' I ask, 'why must we finish?'

John takes the microphone.

Trompeta, Hello and Farewell

'Farewell, Farewell, Trompeta,' he says calmly, methodically.

What? What on earth is going on?

It transpires, as you have already guessed, that *Farewell* is a neighbouring yacht that has been eavesdropping on our conversation, no doubt in stitches over Ruth's and my rookie attempts to use the VHF. The radio is free to use. Only one person can speak at a time on each channel, but anyone can listen in and join in. *Farewell*'s skipper is offering us some fuel for the outboard. Soon, he dinghies over with a can, helps John to fill our outboard tank and replaces the sheared safety pin. I hide below and will be spared my blushes until tomorrow. He disappears.

We join Ruth and Derek for beers, ice cold and enormously welcome, in the nearest bar, a short sandy step from the rickety dinghy dock, and arrange to go for a short sail on Sunday.

The sailing trip was enjoyable. Uneventful. Everyone had an opportunity to helm. Nothing broke. We delivered Ruth and Derek safely to their hotel and continued with our preparations.

Bridget Arregger

Los Roches

Trompeta Sailing Diaries: Monday 4 August 1997

We have spent the night in Laguna Grande which is deserted. We have a large bay to ourselves and have seen only one other yacht since we set out. I stood watching for fish at about 07:00 and later saw a shoal of tiny fish. I don't know how to fish from the stationary boat - would need a float or something to keep the hook away from the hull.

It's lovely here; the landscape is bare red earth alternating with chalky white, with scrubby bushes, cacti and mangroves. There are lots of pelicans and some smaller black birds with forked tails, white beaks and breast, which circle above the trees.

The water seemed blue and clear from a distance, but now that we're stopped, it looks milky due to a suspension of extremely fine white sand.

We had a good swim yesterday. Fortunately we had noticed the strong current straight away as we drifted quite fast away from the boat. We headed back to the ladder at the stern and then swam around the boat against the current up one side and then let the current carry us down the other until we were tired and climbed out quickly. Jan paused to clear some mud off the waterline and came out coated in fine sand all over in a delicate tracery of chevrons. I

Los Roches

photographed a dragonfly on the transom and John asleep in the cockpit.

We set off at 09:00 with mainsail and jib up, heading for Chimanana Grande, but at 11:20, we put the engine on as there was no wind. At 15:00, we were not getting anywhere, so we changed course for Caracas del Oeste and Este, where there is supposed to be good anchorage and snorkelling. Still haven't caught any fish. I feel faintly seasick. We anchor 17:15 in Caracas del Este.

No reply from Rich, so will send him a new message and one to Nick at Trinity Hall.

To Rich: Have you received Inmarsat 400612 sent on 31 July?

To Nick: Please contact Rich to see if Inmarsat is functioning. We sent a message on Wednesday, but no reply. We need him to cut brass rod for the dinghy sheer pins and send them to Vemasca. He will find the brass rod either on the work bench or in the cupboard under the stairs. 4 mm diameter, round cross-section, cut into 6-inch lengths. Use hacksaw.

Inmarsat is a marine system that works by satellite and radio and doesn't need Internet connection. There is no other connection at sea. The Internet (1983) and the World Wide Web (1991) are in their infancy. We can send brief messages. If my sons can post brass rod to the chandlery in Margarita, we can pick it up when we return to drop Jan and Simon off before we set off up the East Caribbean Island chain.

Tuesday 5 August: Leave at 06:30 and put the mainsail up but no wind so motoring. Nearly out of sight of all land, one island off the port beam. Cooking so far has been easy, with plenty of fresh fruit and veg despite early fear that these would not be readily available. Found okra, cabbage and lots of beans and grains in open bins at the market. Will need to see how to make cornmeal muffins as this is the chief flour. Have been baking bread every couple of days to use up the musty old packets. Kneading dough while the boat is rocking violently is a new skill to be learned. We had scrambled eggs and bacon on toast with butter out of a tin.

Fish still not biting. John suggests we should use different bait, perhaps a spinner. We have tried using plastic fish and squid with large hooks. We have no idea what we should be doing.

Last night's bay was delightful with clean enough water off the beach for snorkelling. I used my goggles and was able to dive down to about 6 ft. and see urchins and fish. Still murky around the boat so could not dive down on the anchor but then we were in over 20 ft. of water, and I can't dive down that deep. The flies were a nuisance, biting sharply, though nothing to show for it. The blisters from my first mosquito bites are still full of liquid - the biggest one burst but seems to be filling with liquid again. Don't know whether to burst them or not, so leave them alone in the faint hope that my body chemistry can sort itself out. I know it is never a good idea to scratch.

John gets stung by a jellyfish, and this makes a nasty wound.

Passing a flock of seabirds crash-diving for fish. Also a dolphin. There were a lot of dolphins each day.

We sailed for a couple of hours. 20 knots of wind. Making 7½ knots, which is excellent. We arrive Playa Caldera, Tortuga, at 16:00. We Need four attempts at anchoring as the anchor keeps dragging. Beautiful turquoise water with patches of dark weeds. We dinghy ashore to explore. Beautiful white sand with coral. Idyllic little island if you are visiting briefly. Janice and Simon wash sheets over the stern. John makes repairs to outer reef points on the mainsail.

Wednesday 6 August: We weigh anchor at 06:00 and hoist the sails at 07:15. There is a NE swell and 12-20 knots of wind. We use the pole to put the foresail out on the opposite side of the boat from the mainsail and goosewing with the wind behind us. John catches some kind of big fish. He is trying to haul it in and calls me to help. I am supposed to hook it with the gaff - a long pole with a vicious hook. But the fish spirals vigorously away, the boat is tipping alarmingly, I am too timid to lean far enough out, and we lose it. We find the fishhook has gone from the line and realise the fish must have broken it off at the thread and still have the hook in its jaw.

This may mean it is in pain and cannot feed - not a nice way to die. Later, using a scrap of raw tomato on a fine hook, I catch a small pretty fish that I identify from the book as a Spanish mackerel: broader and flatter than an English one and with yellow spots on its sides and no stripes. Dark bones. According to the book it is one of the best mackerels, leaner and more delicately flavoured. It flaps about. I bang it on the head. I don't disapprove of the principle of hunting for food, but killing is unpleasant, and I decide this will be the first and last fish that I try to catch. However, having caught it and killed it, I persevere, gut it and fry it gently in oil with the lid on. It doesn't go far between the four of us, but we have one small fillet each as a starter before using the large tin of chicken supreme with added pasta that I found at the back of one of the lockers. That is too stodgy and would be appropriate for cold wet camping conditions in Britain but not the tropics. I suspect it was left over from sailing in England. Feeding four people with several strong dislikes for storable things like cheese, chunky pasta, nuts, olives, UHT milk, beer and mushrooms is not easy. We're all complaining about the heat and don't feel like doing much.

Engine on at 15:00, set course for the short sail to Carenera. John proposed handing it over to me for pilotage and showed me how to plan a course that would safely bring us to a required point, after which I could judge by eye. We arrive there without mishap at 18:30.

Los Roches

Thursday 7 August: That was a long sail yesterday - 11 hours with motoring the last hour and a half. We saw two gulls on a chunk of driftwood that was exactly the right size to take them both, chirping loudly as we passed them. They seemed supremely pleased with themselves. Lots more dolphins, with a baby one.

We are anchored in a sheltered bay and the boat is not rolling much. Compared with the previous bays, it seems dirty and unpleasant with a harsh shoreline. Mangroves are solid down to the water. Their exposed roots harbour many varieties of wildlife but are inhospitable to humans. We are too hot and tired much of the time, but my slight queasiness has passed. Mosquitoes are noisy but none of us has been bitten today. We kept a coil smoking last night.

Our adventure today is to go shopping in Higerote. We find a bus and wait in stifling heat until it is full before it sets off. No bus timetable. All buses run on demand. We reach the main shop, check that we will be able to use a credit card and potter around, filling our baskets. I found some dried beans on special offer that will be useful for a stew. I cannot understand the Spanish label or ask for information, but they look like standard dried beans.

At the tills, they will not accept credit cards after all. Presumably they had not understood. None of us speaks Spanish although John has a smattering of words.

Two of us stay to guard the shopping while the other two go in search of a bank or cash point. While Janice and I are waiting, someone pulls down the shutters of the shop. We must appear horrified but gather from various voluble streams of Spanish and hand gestures that this is for the lunch break. John and Simon come back with cash. We wait for the shop to open again, pay and leave.

We don't have any energy for looking around so wait for a bus back. We take on fuel and water, leave at 18:00 and sail overnight. We have the wind behind us but can't keep to our desired course as we risk gybing, which is the slack boom swinging dangerously fast from one side to the other. We're going at a mere 3 knots, and it is uncomfortably bumpy.

Friday 8 August: I'm on watch early in the morning. There is a steady breeze. I see the sky grow lighter in the East at 05:00. What words can convey the powerful feeling of being alone on deck, no land or other boats in sight?

There is the sea in all directions. There are stars and moon that have been traversing the sky. The aloneness. The beauty. The timeless functioning of the universe.

The depth of the water beneath me. I must not dwell on that. It has a siren call.

Soon there will be sun. I focus on the strength of the wind propelling us efficiently and the ingenuity of the design of the sails keeping us on course. I notice there is a batten loose in the mainsail and rescue it at 05:30 when it is light enough to see properly.

Tigrilla Squid

Trompeta Sailing Diaries: Friday 22 August 1997

We anchored in Ensenada Tigrilla El Oculto at 16:00. A rough translation could be the Bay of the Little Hidden Tiger or the Hidden Bay of the Little Tiger. I don't know the grammar and Google Translate does not help, except to suggest that tigrillo is more likely a lynx or another local wild cat, not a small tiger.

It was a hidden bay and when we arrived, deserted. We did not spy any little wild cats, although we did hear howler monkeys. John is not given to waxing lyrical in the log, but he admits to 'Wonderful location, v. Good snorkelling and reef.'

I wanted to swim every day, all day long. I was growing used to wearing a mask and snorkelling. It was essential to wear a T-shirt, particularly when in the water, to avoid sunburn in these early days. The coral was beautiful and fascinating, and the rocks swarmed with tiny fish in all colours. There was so much to see. So much to take delight in. We could all spend hours exploring underwater.

I discovered a secluded area around the other side of a large coral-covered rock. While I was idling, with my face under the surface, I was approached by three squid - mummy, daddy, baby? - hovering to see what I would do and waving their tendrils at me. We watched each other, mutually curious and friendly. I reached out my hands to them, mimicking their movements with my fingers but we did not touch.

They reminded me of the octopus that fascinated me as a child when my dad worked in the original aquarium in the Citadel on Plymouth Hoe. I would spend hours watching it and it seemed to be scrutinising me. I have since learned that octopuses and squid are highly intelligent and often interact with their keepers when in captivity.

What John does not enter in the log is that on a subsequent visit with the two of us, the bay was again deserted, and we went skinny dipping. We swam about 100 metres to the beach and stretched out on the coral- and shell-strewn sand. We were both accustomed to the sun and no longer burned, provided we used plenty of suncream. Belatedly, we spotted that a yacht had entered the bay and was preparing to anchor. I swam high-speed back to our boat, popped on my swim togs and dived back into the water. I found the three squid in the same place. And again on another visit.

It is my favourite bay in all the Caribbean.

Diving on the Anchor

Trompeta Sailing Diaries: Tuesday 23 December 1997

As we approach Bequia, I am sitting towards the stern on the port side with my legs dangling over the edge. We are tipping over quite a way as we sail at high speed in a strong wind. No one is steering. The yacht is on autohelm and will keep us on course. I'm on 'lookout' duty.

When I search to starboard, I see a small dinghy with an outboard approaching us. A person is standing up and aiming something at us.

I call urgently to John, who pops up into the cockpit and together we watch cautiously as the dinghy bobs about precariously, moving around us. That is, I watch cautiously. John, I notice, is not at all perturbed. As the dinghy comes closer, I can see the man is aiming not a gun but a camera at us. I relax.

Later, the photographer visits us at anchor and shows us the proofs of the photos he has taken. They are good and we order a large copy of one of them.

Anchoring is not easy due to the wind and a shelf that runs across the bay. At this stage, I know little about the principles of anchoring but have learned to stand by the anchor locker in the bow and plop the anchor over at the right moment when instructed. I must then watch as the anchor chain uncoils from where it has been neatly stowed (by me) in the locker.

Instruments show John the depth of water under the keel, and he must calculate how much chain we need. To make this possible, the chain is painted at intervals with bands of colours in the order in which they appear in the rainbow: red, orange, yellow, green, light blue, dark blue, violet (or purple). At five metres, there is one red band. At ten metres, two red bands. At 15 metres, one orange band, 20 metres, two orange and so on up to 70 metres, double purple. It's reasonably easy to remember and if you lose count, numbers ending in five have a single band and those ending in zero have a double band.

I must watch for the faded coloured markers and call the numbers to John as each coloured band enters the water so he knows how much chain is underwater.

A fathom is six feet or a little under two metres. Towards the end of the 19th Century, Samuel Langhorne Clemens chose his pen name from the second, or two-fathom, mark on anchor chains. 'By the mark, twain.'

When the yacht seems stable, someone must dive down and check that the anchor is properly embedded in the sand. This is miserable in dirty marinas but can be enjoyable in clean, clear water.

Diving on the Anchor

Bequia is clean, but there is an inadequate coating of sand on the ridge in Admiralty Bay in Port Elizabeth and the anchor slides on the smooth rock below. There is no need to dive yet; we can feel the anchor dragging. After two hours of futile attempts, we move to a different anchorage in an awkward place, jealous of the *cats* that can pull up onto the beach. We need at least 6 ft. or 2 metres of water.

I have never tried diving down more than about 6 ft. in British swimming pools. Here, I find I can dive down easily with my mask and snorkel, holding my breath long enough to check that the anchor is firmly embedded in sand and gravel. It should hold overnight. I see that our keel is considerably more than two metres above the bottom.

A year later, in Bonaire, we found a scuba diving school. John asked me if I'd like to learn. Yes, I would. It must be fun to go deep. I imagined a helmet and hoses and some sort of deep-sea pressure arrangement. So innocent!

Scuba diving uses the same mask and snorkel as in shallow water, but the snorkel tube is connected to a tank of air on your back. No helmet! You can remove the tube from your mouth and hold your breath as with snorkelling or pop it in and breathe underwater. Clever huh? You wear weights around your waist to keep you underwater. Without weights, you can't help floating in salt water. Diving is easy.

Bridget Arregger

I am so busy concentrating I forget that my ears will hurt. They don't. I see a seahorse. I am as happy as Larry (whoever he is) and I received my first PADI (Professional Association of Diving Instructors) certificate.

I discovered that John had ulterior motives for sweetly encouraging me to learn to dive. We have tanks and weights on board, and he'd like me to be able to clean the underneath of the hull.

The devastating Hurricane *'Wrong Way Lenny'* in 1999 destroyed much of the familiar coastlines of the Caribbean islands.

I have *Googled* 'Happy as Larry'. Remarkable.

Three Trees and Somebody Tief de Gas.

Today's Wordle solution was CEDAR, and this has given me the inspiration for this month's story. Our topic is 'tree'.

Suppose, one day, I put in METER and have three Yellows and a Green. The second E is in the correct place, the first E, the T and the R are in the wrong places and the M is not included. TREE would be an obvious choice by moving the T to first place, followed by the R. But TREE has four letters and Wordle needs five and never uses plurals. The answer is clear as there is only one other option, THREE. This has set my mind wandering and brought back memories. Three things stand out: one, the beautiful ancient cedar at Missenden Abbey where I attended various weekend teacher training courses; two, the equally ancient cedar at Dartington Hall that is propped up by iron stakes, usually omitted by artists; and three, the patois in the Caribbean where 'th' is pronounced 't.' Hence, three would sound like a tree. One, two, tree.

One of my memorable incidents while sailing was getting drunk on rum punches. It was Monday, 29 December 1997, the evening that we had drinks at Dennis' Hideaway in Mayreau, the smallest inhabited island in St Vincent and the Grenadines. We had celebrated Christmas in Bequia and sailed to Mayreau via Canouan. Our British friend Annie was crewing with us, and we were buddy sailing with Dutch friends Jan and Adriana on yacht Bonte Koe (Spotted Cow). We were a merry bunch and Dennis' Hideaway was a favourite of the yachting community and came highly recommended. With our self-appointed local guide, we had climbed the steep cliff paths past various fishing family houses and a scattering of goats and chickens. We reckoned you must be able to live simply and cheaply in the Caribbean with a few goats and chickens and plenty of fish and mango trees.

I had not yet discovered the potency of rum punches in a land where rum is cheap and the imported cartons of orange juice inordinately expensive. I had three rums with a hint of orange juice, no more than anyone else, but I was disconcertingly unsteady as we all scrambled our way down the steep uneven path in the dark to where we were promised a dinghy ride back out to our yachts anchored in Saltwhistle Bay. Our guide and dinghy operator tried to start his outboard engine, but it wouldn't fire. He exchanged rapid patois with his various companions in other dinghies and then explained to us, 'Somebody tief de gas.' One of the others took us back to our respective yachts (or he borrowed a dinghy. I didn't know or care). Back on board, I was copiously sick, to everyone's amusement.

The next day, we sailed to Tobago Cays and then back to Saline Bay in Mayreau for New Year's Eve. We were never in a hurry to go anywhere but meandered back and forth as we heard of appealing places to visit as we made our way up the island chain.

Prompt: tree, in any interpretation.

Dartington Hall – an Imagined Visit

I go to Dartington Hall and into the gardens, another haunt of childhood. A local amateur art group is settling down to paint and I watch them fuss and fidget as they decide where to sit.

Some settle quickly, not straying far from the gate, others choose buildings, yet others, statues, some the long flower border. They all place their flimsy folding chairs with apparent care. However, there are some who sit in such an awkward way they must twist their heads repeatedly between looking at their paper and their chosen view. I itch to go over and help them find a better orientation so they can see their drawing and the view at the same time. One has made the obvious choice and picked the spectacular old cedar supported with wire braces. He works quickly. Most likely influenced by some romantic notion of non-technological perfection, he leaves out the braces in his preliminary sketch.

No one is in the places I would choose. Places which reveal a hidden corner, a tiny natural treasure. They are going for something grand: trying too hard and not trying hard enough. They haven't learned to listen and observe, and their paintings cannot help but be banal, lifeless and familiar. There is no magic in their lives and there will be no magic in their paintings.

Someone says hello and asks if I like art and what medium I prefer.

'Oils' I say, 'with a knife.'

I gesture with my arms and my whole body to demonstrate deftly applying the paint to make confident, bold marks. The woman says, 'How nice,' with tight lips and a disapproving frown. Her work shows she is a precise and careful water-colourist, of the kind I do not admire, neat and with no flair, which I expect will sell satisfactorily in the local tourist shops. I must frame some more of my smaller ones and put them for sale. But I must find the right galleries. Neither her paintings nor mine would be presented at their best if placed side by side.

I sit on stone steps behind a little fountain with a pair of stone swans, letting the silence descend on me like velvet, smothering me and filling my ears. Little by little, tiny sounds creep in: a grasshopper close by my feet, a rustle of leaves behind me. I begin to hear the birdsong. I let peace envelop me, absorb into me, and spread through me. I sit for a long time.

A man is climbing the stone steps towards me. He is looking from left to right, walking slowly, and obviously enjoying the flowers and trees. He smiles and says hello as he passes.

I smile back, but my mood is disturbed. I leave the gardens. One member of the art group is arriving late as I reach the courtyard. She walks in grandly, carrying her folding chair and a shoulder bag of paper and paints. She had more important things to do than go to class on time.

Writing is . . .

Writing is . . .

Making biscuits

Throw in the ingredients as they materialise

Unbidden

From dark recesses

Stir thoroughly

Let it rest

Shape the dough, Peel the trimmings, Scrape the bowl

I ice

With curlicues and swirls, silver balls

You eat the icing separately

Spit the hard silver balls into the fire

Lest they detract,

distract from the wholemeal, whole meal

Saving the substance, the essence

till last.

Bridget Arregger

You're a Natural Poet

You're a natural poet who's stuck.

The words do not come, no such luck.

You seek metre and rhyme,

Search for free verse sublime,

But even your limericks suck.

When I am busily writing

my house begins to rot

go to pot

when I am not so hot,

and have lost the plot,

then I can clean the lot

or not

Jersey Saltram

My name is Jersey Saltram. You are bound to ask so I will jump in and tell you there are two reasons for being named after an item of clothing. One, I am the unplanned result of a late-in-life visit to the Channel Islands by my parents and two, my hair at birth was a soft fawn brown colour with charcoal highlights, reminiscent of a Jersey cow, my mother's favourite farmyard animal. Thirdly, my father came from a family of Saltrams of some note. I neither know nor care of what note.

Jersey has been an interesting name to live with and has given rise to various nicknames, as you can imagine. I favour Jumpers or Cashmere. I do not like Pullover, called out in a police-like tone accompanied by a mock siren. Or Pushover. You can guess what would be associated with Sweater.

I tend to be the centre of attention for a few minutes in any new group and then discarded in favour of someone else if I don't immediately deliver the goods. I guess this explains my habit of taking the stage briefly and glorying in it, life and soul, then vanishing without warning or trace when I'm bored.

You will see that today I am wearing my favourite orange dungarees with a purple sweatshirt. I also have red jeans and a burgundy hoodie. I love vibrant, clashing colours and being flamboyant, which I alternate with grey and navy on self-effacing, private days. Do I dodge into a telephone box to change? Maybe.

I do not like to be type-cast or pigeon-holed. I'm not going to tell you if I am male or female. I am what youngsters today call non-binary when they do not want to be defined by their biological sex or live according to others' gender expectations.

Prompt: create a character's name from a pet name and a street name.

On the Spectrum

'Thirty-nine ice creams and an ice lolly please.'

'Good morning. We have exactly thirty-nine flavours,' the Baskin and Robbins assistant replied as she raised the shutter. 'It used to be thirty-one, but we've added a few. Would you like one of each?'

She smiled to herself as she surveyed the long line of schoolchildren. Let them sort it out themselves, she thought. She would scoop out one of each into separate cones. She predicted much shrieking and fighting as each child expressed a preference, and no one knew which was which. Thirty-nine flavours, from vanilla through every imaginable fruit to caramel, cookies 'n' cream, mint chocolate chip, coconut, pistachio almond, rum raisin to liquorice. No room here for the whole 1000. No ginger. No eggs & bacon or curry. She knew there were ice cream houses around the world where you could order any flavour you could dream up and they would produce it for you. Her own favourite was her mother's homemade delicate cardamom kulfi.

The leader of the children nodded.

'Just a moment I'll fetch some trays.' She returned with a pile of small cardboard trays, each with six holes, the right size for taking an ice cream cone.

She set the first tray in a holder beside the till, positioned six empty cones and carefully added a scoop of ice cream to each one, handed the filled tray to the leader, then started filling the next tray. As the leader passed out each tray to eager hands, the assistant loaded the next, moving along the brightly coloured deep tubs of ice cream. Taking her time, she savoured the range of fragrances as she disturbed the early morning unbroken surfaces of the pots and was disappointed when she had counted out all thirty-nine. This was an unusual request and broke the monotony of her summer job.

'And the ice lolly?' she added, looking up at the young leader, 'Is that for you? What would you like? It's on the house. You deserve it.'

'Thanks,' said the young leader, 'I'll have a plain orange one, please, and I'd like it here, please, not in the house.'

'Not a Funny Feet or a Rocket?'

'No thanks.'

'Fruit pastilles?'

'No.'

'Solero vanilla ice cream with orange sorbet?'

The leader shook their head. It was not clear if this was a young man or a woman.

On the Spectrum

'Twister pineapple and lime with strawberry surprise? That's the best seller.'

'No, thank you. Plain orange please.'

'How about an orange Calippo? That's next in popularity.'

'I want a plain orange. Um. If you have one. Um. Please.' They struggled with their words.

'Calippo is plain orange. You'll like it.'

'How do you know what I like?' The teenager looked puzzled. 'You don't know me.'

'No, but. . .,' the assistant hesitated, 'but it's very popular. Everyone likes them.'

'I'm not everyone.' And, as it seemed more was needed and an explanation, 'Hello, I'm Chris. I'm in charge for half an hour. It's my challenge for today. I'm on the spectrum.'

'On the spectrum,' the assistant echoed. 'That sounds interesting, like the colours of the ice creams. There's orange in the spectrum. Red, orange, yellow . . .'

'Not *that* spectrum,' Chris said with a frown.

Chris accepted the orange Calippo doubtfully but then smiled.

It is nice, thanks. I do like it. You were right.'

As they both turned to survey the children and the anticipated riot, they were surprised to find the ice cream cones had all been sorted and a happy band of youngsters was busy licking and munching.

'Who had the liquorice?' the assistant called out.

'I did,' said one, 'see my mouth.' The mouth was opened wide, and a dark greyish-purple tongue thrust out. There was a chorus of yuck and urgh and eew. It was a far cry from the attractive pale blue of the original ice cream.

'Goodbye Chris, goodbye all,' the assistant said after every child had stepped forward to pay their exact money. Someone had planned this carefully, she thought. She wondered what spectrum Chris meant.

Prompt:39 ice creams and an ice lolly

Skipping

I'm teaching myself to skip. I'm about five or six, I guess. I know I could read my Robin comic while we were renting that house, while we waited for the sitting tenant to leave our proper house. I worried that the postman would not know where to deliver the Robin when we moved.

The garden is long and narrow, small but big enough for a five- or six-year-old, fenced on both sides. There are uneven paving slabs in a line down the middle. There is rough, unkempt grass on the left, perhaps a tree of some kind, too big to notice, and muddy earth with various plants on the right as you look from the back door.

I have a small patch of earth of my own where my mother has tried to teach me how to grow shallots. Mum called them shallots, but I think they were spring onions. They were tiny with green stems. I wanted to learn and have liked gardening, in a fine-weather way, ever since.

My sister and first brother have never been interested. My second brother, born much later, and his wife are keen gardeners. My children and grandchildren? Not interested. When my sons were small, I could snatch some time alone by gardening. They knew that if they came out to pester me, they would be given something useful to do. My initial motive was to kindle a love of the garden. They thought otherwise.

Bridget Arregger

I can't remember what else was growing but I imagine my mother grew other things like leeks, maybe, as she was Welsh, and carrots and celery. I believe she explained to me about heaping soil around the leeks and celery stems so they would stay white. I think there may have been red tulips. Her favourite flowers were red carnations and gladioli, but I don't think there were any of those. Dad would occasionally buy some for her. She would have grown everything in rows, running across, about two or three feet in length from the path to the side fence, and not particularly straight or neat.

Dad would have wanted them straight and neat, but he didn't help with gardening until they moved to Canada. I don't think Mum was a keen gardener but there was no garden at the other house, and I expect she tried to make the most of this one while she could.

There is a wall at the bottom of the garden and a small fig tree. It has figs, but they are small and hard, not nice to eat. Next to the fig tree, there is a gate out into a lane. I don't think I was allowed to go out of the gate, or perhaps it was kept locked. I have no memory of the lane.

Lots of snails live on the crumbling stone wall, and I can remember thinking they would be horrid to eat, although I knew that some people eat snails. Sometimes, I collect the snails and move them to other places in the garden and watch them.

Skipping

The wall is old stone. It is not beautiful. It is patched with concrete and pieces of brick and cinder block, messy and deteriorating. The stones are haphazard not fitted expertly together. There are holes partially filled with uninteresting half-dead weeds and jagged corners. The wall would have been improved if Aubretia or other colourful rock plants could have been encouraged.

I can't visualise the individual pieces, but I imagine there may have been a mixture of the local stones, limestone, flint, slate, quartz and perhaps some granite. Properly constructed, these can have attractive faces, colours, and shapes like dry-stone walls and granite tors on Dartmoor. I remember the multitude of different pebbles at Tinside. I like pebbles. I am drawn by (and like to draw) natural rock formations and am fascinated by the patterns and shapes.

The unevenness of the paving keeps catching the rope, but I persevere and eventually manage enough to feel I can show off to my sister, who has been teasing me about not being able to skip.

Prompt: describe a wall.

Bridget Arregger

Creative Acrostic

Creative activities appeal to mE

Recently, I have been learning about improV

Extemporisation, I feel, will come more easily in a jacuzzI

Ad-libbing is better when relaxed and letting the mind drifT

Then daily pressures don't interfere with inventive phenomenA

Inner thoughts and feelings can rise to the surfacE

Vacant mentality can foster the rich imaginings of a writeR

Eventually, dialogue comes pouring in, authentic and artistiC

Prompt: write an acrostic poem with the initial letters of each line forming the word CREATIVE. I chose to make the end letters form CREATIVE in reverse order as well.

Bicycle Surprise

There has been one notable surprise gift in my life. When I was fifteen my parents gave me a bicycle.

I couldn't ride a bike and hadn't expressed interest or asked for one. I hadn't enjoyed riding my trike when I was small as I hated going down and up kerbs when crossing the road, much to my father's annoyance (I imagine), as I insisted on getting off the trike, wrestling it down to the road, wheeling it slowly across, going round to the front to lift it up onto the pavement and getting awkwardly on again.

My father was a patient man. He never made unreasonable demands. However, I knew that what I was doing must have been annoying. I was annoyed with myself.

At that time, I called the pavement 'mink'. I don't know why, but when my father, mildly exasperated, asked me why, I said emphatically, 'I have to call it MINK because I can't say PAVE MENT.' Dad didn't laugh, but I flushed with surprise and embarrassment and never called it mink again. I guess I muttered pavement under my breath for the rest of the walk. These days, I find I refer to sidewalks or pedestrian walkways. I've spent a lot of time in America and Canada, where 'pavement' means the paved (tarmacked) road where the cars and buses go.

Bridget Arregger

Aged seven, at Butlins in Dublin, where we were staying after my Mother's sister's wedding, when I'd been a bridesmaid and won the Little Princess silver cup dressed in my bridesmaid green dress with lily of the valley posy and white sandals, later dyed sensible brown for school, my father had borrowed a full-sized bicycle and tried to teach me to ride it. It was huge and heavy, with a crossbar. He lifted me on and tried to encourage me to peddle while he hung on to the saddle. It was a disaster. Nothing more was said or done about it. My parents were patient, but I was slow to learn anything that required me to take my feet off *terra firma*.

However, my mother had the bright idea of giving me a bicycle at fifteen so I could take my wet weather gear to the sailing club each Thursday evening to have sailing lessons in much less time than it took to walk. I didn't want to sail but it was my parents' second passion after cycling. They rode a tandem in wartime and toured the country - in the dark, with no road signs. By all accounts, they were extremely proud of this accomplishment. I forget how many times my father pointed out the Swan pub in Moreton in Marsh where they stayed once. When my sister was born, they fitted a sidecar for her. Mercifully, this had disappeared before I became aware of its existence. There is a photo. I submitted to sailing lessons as I couldn't come up with a better way of spending Thursday evenings.

Bicycle Surprise

Dutifully, I set out to ride the bike. After trials in our quiet street, practising taking one hand off to signal, I ventured out onto bigger roads. All went uneventfully until I crossed a wide junction. There must have been loose grit or a sudden noise. I slipped and fell, grazing my knee.

A man rescued me and insisted on walking me home. He said he was a French/Italian waiter in the hotel at the junction. Told me he wrote poetry. Wanted to meet me again.

I can't remember what I said or did or how often we met, but I knew this was not a good idea and somehow got rid of him.

After relaying this event to my parents, showing them the poem he wrote for me, and telling them I preferred to walk to the sailing club, the bike vanished as unexpectedly as it had appeared.

Years later, I came across a piece of research about people who struggled to learn to ride a bike, saying they had not crawled on all fours as a child. When I questioned my mother, she said I had never crawled but sat still or shuffled on my bum until I learned to walk. Lack of crawling, the research suggested, means that the left and right sides of the brain do not co-ordinate fully. A good way to develop coordination is to learn to juggle, the researcher promised. So, as an adult, I set out to learn to juggle. This, I much enjoyed but never learned to feel comfortable on a pushbike. However, I learned enough to ride a motorbike. That will do.

Bridget Arregger

Morgan

Morgan (not his real name) was a tall, muscular lad. Black. West Indian, from St Vincent. I met him when he was a 14-year-old student in the Secondary Modern where I was a brand-new teacher. Morgan wasn't much bothered by learning. I had a lot to learn.

At the end of my first lesson, five minutes before the bell was due, Morgan decided he wanted to leave the room. I stood between him and the door. I was worried about the trouble I would be in if I let him out and terrified of what he might do to me if I didn't. I stood my ground with my back against the door.

Morgan towered over me. He subjected me to a torrent of abuse. Morgan's vocabulary was far from impoverished. I had never heard such rich and inventive phrases concerning female anatomy and women's place in society. I don't think he repeated himself.

When the bell rang, I opened the door and stood aside. Morgan and the rest of the class filed out in silence.

The following morning, Morgan sought me out and politely apologised. 'It won't happen again,' he said. He was true to his word. He worked steadily and quietly from that day on. I had clearly passed some kind of test. I learned later he was constantly in trouble in his other classes and his father and a couple of uncles were in prison. I doubt if I was able to help him much, but he helped me, and I remember him with affection.

Bridget Arregger

Garden Fairies

The garden fairies exchanged looks. Marigold groaned.

Poppy grinned, 'Come on,' she said, 'we can do this. It's not as bad as it looks.'

'Where shall we start?' Bluebell asked, 'All I can see are brambles.'

'And weeds,' Marigold said.

'And moss!' someone else chipped in.

'We'll start how we always do,' Poppy said, taking charge for once, 'one step at a time.' Usually, one of the others was boss but they all looked so dejected, particularly Marigold who was often the leader. Poppy thought she'd better take over for the moment.

'Come on Hazel,' she said, 'you're the strongest. Why don't you start at one end of the biggest bramble patch? Take two others with you to hold the brambles up while you cut and two more to clear away the sections you cut. Holly, gather yourself a posse and start the other end. You can race to see who gets to the middle first. Don't worry about the roots; someone can dig those later; you need to clear the top. While they're doing that, we need a team to sort out the compost. Under all the muddle there are several sections with sturdy partitions. First, we need to clear away the mess that's been dumped on top so we can see what's what. One section should be mature by now and ready to spread. As soon as it's empty, we can start loading new stuff in. We'll need a chain gang.

Who'd like to do that huge tangle of wild roses? Rose and Daffodil? Great! Find yourselves a working party. And remember, whatever you do, don't start cutting from the inside or the whole lot will fall on you!'

'Why are we doing this,' Snowdrop asked.

'Like I've told you,' Poppy said, 'she's a special person. It's not her fault it's been allowed to deteriorate like this. She's been good to us all her life. Now it's our turn to repay her. She turned to Marigold. 'What would you like to do?' she asked.

'I don't know,' said Marigold. 'I've never seen anything like this.

'What do you like doing best when you're not in charge?'

'I don't know. Something small, I guess.'

'Why don't you do one of the pots,' suggested Poppy. 'You'll soon get into it.'

'That's a good idea,' said Marigold. 'Small and manageable.'

'Where's Ivy?' Poppy called out. 'And Columbine? Ah, good. Guess what you're going to do! And who's for the nettles and ground elder?'

Poppy surveyed the multitude of fairies as they flew from place to place. It was hard to see any pattern in what they were doing, especially as most of them transformed each task into a game. But they were good at their jobs and there was plenty of time. Poppy grinned again and joined Marigold and together they worked their way through the collection of pots.

They would leave one or two little finishing touches for the new owner. When she arrived, she would never guess what had been going on.

Prompt: Pick a book at random off your bookshelf and use the title. I picked out Robert Preston's How do we fix this mess?

My Garden in Autumn

Everyone says how lovely my garden is.

Welcoming. Like coming home.

When John and I first walked through the gate past the *For Sale* sign, we looked at each other and smiled. We both felt it. Our first proper home together after our lifetimes of wandering.

It's big. Open. With three grassy spaces, on different levels, too small for meadows, too unkempt for lawns, with a roly-poly slope, divested of thistles, waiting for grandchildren. A plum tree at the corner of the house invites young climbers. There are no flowers at this time of year as I have not learned what to plant. No sudden patches of bright colour to catch the eye. No cultivated borders.

The whole garden is enclosed by high banks, rich with subtle colour; young golden elm not yet ravaged by fungus-raddled beetles; ancient apple heavy with nibbled green fruit; damson and greengage; deep purple almond and copper beech; self-seeded ash and maple, turning, falling for shuffling leaf therapy; feathery white willow seeds catching the breezes, dark red haws and hips waiting for winter birds.

Alive. With small birds. The night calls of owls. Bats narrowly avoid brushing your ears and your hair. One huge lime: embracing; hiding, in summer, the remains of a swing, not yet realised. Moth-eaten pine with magpies' nest, stolen noisily from rooks, painstakingly rebuilt last spring, nursery for a foolish fat chick, not yet wanting to fly. Flight of stone steps going nowhere but up, the folly of some previous occupant, Jacob's ladder, littered with unswept leaves.

A deep well, surrounded but not guarded by flagstones too heavy for me to shift, needing a wall and grating for when the grandchildren are stronger than me, but, perhaps, not yet as cautious. Seeds of iris, poker, peony, dock. Tangles, above and below ground, of honeysuckle, bindweed, periwinkle, and bramble. The occasional rabbit. Stoat. Fox. Frog underfoot. Grass Snake, warm, in the compost heap. One year a Hoopoe. Another year, a pair of pheasants looking for a suitable nesting place, perhaps. Familiar neighbourly evening tabby cat, watching for voles. One clovered and plantained area is riddled with field mouse tracks and woven tunnels. The dry-stone wall is cracking, undermined by warren and Buddleia. No moles. Yet. Nettles on the steepest banks, out of my reach. Good for butterflies but also lying in wait for agile, unsuspecting grandchildren. I will need help in clearing them now John has gone.

My refuge.

Wild. Safe.

Like John.

Needing, perhaps, but not wanting refinement.

From Cotswolds to East Midlands

I miss my garden and the Cotswold Water Park but the landscape here is open, hilly countryside with good views and the Grand Union Canal is some compensation.

The dogs and I walk once or twice a day for about an hour: my trousers tucked into walking shoes, arms covered to protect from brambles, thistles and nettles where the paths have become overgrown. I reported one footpath to the County Council and two days later a narrow strip had been cleared. I can't imagine it was the Council - it was too soon - so it was probably one of the locals. I reported it again later and had a friendly call from the Council and it has now been properly cleared. Marvellous! The path is a popular one from the village centre to the train station. Popular for dog walkers - the station road is more direct for commuters in a hurry and easier for cases on wheels.

After the completely flat terrain in the Water Park, the hills were difficult at first, but I hardly notice them now and can see them for the gentle slopes they are. There is one grand walk - about two hours strolling with inquisitive dogs who like to investigate every pee-mail (as Laura calls them) - up Station Road to the church, over a couple of stiles into the fields, fraternise with familiar dogs, walk smartly past the unfamiliar, unfriendly ones, trudge uphill to the old barn, admire the view, notice how two windmills line up so it looks like one windmill with six blades, perfectly synchronised, dodge inside the barn to capture a photo of the view through a hole in the old stone wall, over another stile, skip down the next field and head left alongside several fields of heady sneeze-inducing rape to the tiny arched stone footbridge over the junction of two streams. The banks are too steep for my cautious puppies to climb down for a drink, and I promise them I'll bring water next time.

I see and hear the train come past on the slow line from Birmingham to London as I saunter along the next stretch of straight open path alongside wheat fields and the puppies start a race. They are 50 yards ahead of me, turn and race back, narrowly missing my legs. They do this, as if demented, a few times, then contentedly sniff their way along at more leisurely pace until we reach the small, reclaimed park that used to be a rubbish dump. It's a local volunteer project and is populated with trees and seats with memorial plaques. There's a stream, a pond, a bird-hide and a small fragrant wildflower meadow.

For the walk back we take the hidden overgrown paths that skirt the village - muddy in winter, brambly in summer - down a cul-de-sac, behind the pub, alongside the muddy cow field, fighting our way through the undergrowth, and emerge nearly home for a final sedate walk with correct slack-lead walking and kerb drill, through the new-build estate to our home and garden.

From Cotswolds to East Midlands

The cow field leads to a longer walk down to the Grand Union, along the tow path and back in a big loop. We haven't managed the whole walk yet. One time, when we tried, a section of the path was obscured by head-height summer weeds, and we couldn't find the way. But, since then, we have discovered the footbridge over the stream and walked as far as the motorway bridge occasionally. And we have visited the canal a few times via the main road. It's been cool and shady by the water in the latest heat wave, and we pause to watch the narrow boats going through the numerous locks. Friends who have owned narrow boats call it indolent gongoozling if I don't offer to help. The puppies wear harnesses in case I need to fish them out.

There are fields, footpaths and bridleways in all directions. It's easy to take the dogs for a walk off the lead and since the cluster of five windmills alongside the A5 and the neighbouring pair close to home by the railway are visible for miles, it is hard to get lost.

Bridget Arregger

God knows

When I was a child I thought as a child,

spoke as a child,

to the fairies,

but did not tell my parents, who would have poured scorn on such silliness,

wrote letters to Father Christmas,

but hid them from parents who did not believe in him,

prayed to God,

but in secret as my parents, predictably, did not believe in him either and

forbade me to go to church so I could grow up with a mind of my own.

I went to church

because my friends did and because defying authority came naturally and because Eve was a good role model and because my parents, not being God, were not aware of my transgressions,

though they made me aware of my nakedness by flaunting their own.

God knows

When I grew up and became a woman, I put away these childish things,

but kept pictures of fairies, said thank you for presents,

but not to Father Christmas

and avoided going to church for many years.

But I cannot put away God.

My universe does not yet have room for a supernatural being who created it,

and cares about it.

Strangely, believing in a creator is no more difficult than not.

Being here is the strangest thing of all,

but someone who cares?

A supernatural caring parent? I wish.

When the traffic lights turn to red as I approach, do I blame the traffic lights?

Bridget Arregger

If the rain wets my washing, do I blame the rain?

No, I don't.

Do I blame the god who makes the rain? No.

Or thank god for the sun? Hmm. I have been heard to say, 'thank god!'

When I die, will I go to the next world?

That is immensely appealing.

I want to know what is beyond this one.

But would I have to die again to see what is beyond the next?

And beyond the next world? And the next?

If there is no end; if there was, perhaps, no beginning, what is there?

Jesus was real. He cared. He was a teacher more than a parent.

I invite him to sit in an empty chair and tell him about things that upset me.

I cry.

To Jesus, I say, thank you …, sorry …, please …. A teaspoon of prayer. It helps to say my thoughts out loud.

God knows

Or write them down.

If Jesus is the son of God and we are all the children of God
what then is God?

Does God stand for Good?

Does God stand for the collective efforts of good people?

For the understanding of the difference between good

and not so good,

for falling short of targets?

Does God stand for the underlying laws of the universe?

For the wisdom that we seek when we explore all possibilities
through the arts, literature, theatre, history, philosophy, the natural
sciences, metaphysics?

Does God stand for anything more than wishful thinking?

Does any of this matter?

Who cares?

God knows.

Bridget Arregger

Beehives and Biohazards

Love in the time of COVID: Cassie

Cassie rolled over sleepily and reached for the swab to take her daily saliva test. She took her temperature, punched in her code, reported she felt physically normal and closed her eyes for a few more minutes before the alarm sounded again. When she had showered and dressed, she drew back the curtains and opened the simulated window view, selected her favourite moorland within the permitted 20 miles of travel, and gazed out at the live video panorama, trying to spot the skylark she could hear. She loved the moors and walked whenever possible. She was lucky she had found a vacancy here rather than in one of the distant city blocks.

The window-framed screen occupied a large expanse of wall, and it seemed as if you could lean out and breathe in the fresh air. No doubt one day the more expensive models would include the smells. An extensive range of views from all over the world was available, with live transmission beamed down by satellite. It was possible to download views from Space. The live view was satisfyingly realistic if limited. For a truly breath-taking experience a virtual reality headset was needed.

Beehives and Biohazards

Her single occupancy flat was light and airy – pleasant, despite being artificially lit and ventilated, and with no outside walls. Like all apartments in the intensive new build blocks, rapidly created to isolate when necessary and accommodate all displaced persons from long-term homeless and refugees to recently bankrupt, it was an open plan hexagon, part of an elaborate, close-knit, space-saving honeycomb. The architecture, derived from earlier geodesic designs and modelled on natural wild beehives, had won various awards. The building was composed of ready-made modules, fitted together like Lego; quick, cheap, and easy to construct, which made alterations and extensions possible and allowed for a range of apartments to suit different family sizes. Roof sections faced in all possible directions, with solar panels getting the maximum input.

Cassie had opted for a limited palette of natural colours and chosen a variety of partitions to separate the floor space into different living areas. She slid aside delicately decorated Japanese-style paper-thin, fire-proof screens and entered her kitchen area. She prepared crushed mixed beans on toast and coffee, checked her *Who'sIn* messages and settled down with the news on her portable screen. She could have ordered something from the assigned patisserie, but she liked to manage for herself and had requested a fully equipped kitchen. She ate privately, enjoying the moorland scenery, not in the mood for joining her friendship group in the online chat room. Those friends could wait until after work.

Bridget Arregger

She supplemented her universal income with the bonus she received for a designated hazardous job in recycling. She topped it up further with sales of jewellery created from items she could retrieve. Apart from leasing the latest in VR, her needs were simple. That was not a bad thing as she was finding most consumer goods were no longer available. Not all agreed, but perhaps most goods were not right for a world in indefinite lockdown, which would continue while new viruses continued to appear and mutate at a rate that vaccines could not match.

The unregulated capitalism of the past was no longer workable and there was ongoing debate about what must replace it. Community-led cooperatives were popular. They provided choice with all the pleasure of developing new skills without the daily grind of having to do the same arduous things every day.

Everyone she knew received the universal income and few people wasted efforts in trying to exceed it by any great amount. Among her friends, those with valued skills and creative enterprise found their rewards in the pleasure of their creativity and recognition by their peers. The hoarding of wealth in the form of accumulation of goods and an ostentatious lifestyle was possible but many found that laughable. Her modest extra earnings enabled her to have greater choice over furnishings and, if she had wanted it, a wider range of clothing. It would have afforded her an exterior room with a natural view of the surroundings, but she preferred the greater variety of the televised scenes. Cassie, like many others, was content to save her credit for something in the future. She would have liked to travel but, like everyone else, had to content herself with virtual reality.

Checking her diary, she noted this evening's community service was on the vegetable allotments. For work on the allotments, she was paid in kind. She made sure she kept up a good supply of coffee and a variety of chilli and other peppers in the sun-warmed tropical greenhouses. For tomorrow, she had scheduled herself for milking, a task she particularly enjoyed since she had acquired some skill. The early days had been comical. She had now made friends with all the goats and was especially fond of Betty who had been the naughtiest while Cassie was learning to milk her and had usually kicked over the bucket more than once. Cassie liked to help with milking at least once a week and was happy to volunteer if someone had tested positive and was in quarantine. The goats and sheep were free to roam on common land. They would be rounded up by the earlier team.

Community service suited Cassie so long as she could pick outdoor tasks. She avoided indoor jobs as much as possible. Cleaning windows was one of her bugbears, so it was perhaps fortunate that there were few windows to clean. Oddly enough, she reflected, she didn't mind mucking out the animals, whereas she hated cleaning toilets. Someone had to do the dirty jobs, and the universal income did not come without obligations, but most people knuckled down and got on with it. It was possible to *almost* meet your quota with things you liked doing. There were enough people on each block for the less favoured tasks to come round only occasionally.

She saw she had requested a slot on the early morning rota for hillwalking in two days' time. She'd forgotten to confirm. She should have confirmed the booking ages ago.

Guarding her identity, she surreptitiously checked to see if Sam would be going. Hmm. Their name did not come up. She could still hope. They need not have confirmed yet. She wondered if they would search for her name. They'd met twice on the hillwalking rota but although she was pretty sure they felt the same attraction, it was early days and they had not yet exchanged details of their regular leisure activities.

She skimmed through the options in the window view and picked a route with a special appeal, hoping it would have a vacancy. She was lucky. She checked the weather forecast, entered her code, and ordered a set of garments and walking boots that would arrive freshly cleaned and sanitised later in the day.

She enjoyed her long country walks. Moreover, among the available pursuits, all with monitored social-distancing, hillwalking was one of the best for meeting people who also liked to spend as much time as possible outdoors.

Ah well, it was time to go to work. She fetched her biohazard suit and the key to her bicycle, tapped in her code and her preferred route and requested permission to leave.

Bridget Arregger

Lottery

Love in the Time of COVID: Stud

Simon (Stud) Studley dragged himself across his cell and sat stroking the sore places where the chains had chafed and some sore places untouched by chains. His keepers would be in later to massage his ankles with soothing cream. They would offer to assist with the other places too.

He knew he was in a prison previously used for male sex offenders but as there were no longer any of those, or any male offenders, it was otherwise empty apart from his two attentive female guards. There were bars on the windows and heavy doors on either side of the standard 'airlock' arrangement. To prevent him from escaping, no doubt, but more importantly to keep him safe from being 'rescued.' There were many women outside who would wish to spring him. Ever since the latest chromosome-related virus had wiped out more than 99% of males world-wide, he was in no doubt that he was better off inside.

It was not a hard life. But not easy either: his balls ached. All of him ached. Once, he would have dreamed of this life as a utopia. But many times lately, he had had to find alternative ways to keep the prize winners happy, despite the copious supply of Viagra, and felt he was no better than a woman. Yet, he was still prized. That gave him some satisfaction, he supposed.

Fetch!

Doggy Tails

Where'd it go, Loki?

What? I look at her expectantly and wag my tail.

Where'd it go, Loki? Where's the ball? Get the ball.

The ball! Get the ball! I put my head on one side and then started patrolling the garden. I didn't see her throw it – could be anywhere. I run purposefully. It may seem random to her, but I'm following all the trails of where it's been in the last hour.

How about over here by the gravel path? What can I find? Cat pee? Hmm. Voles recently. Old poo – mine or Arianna's? Definitely Arianna's and there's Arianna's pee. Focus! Where's the ball?

Here's a ball. Nope, not the right one; it looks the same but that's not the one she was throwing. Doesn't smell the same. Come on Arianna don't stand there in your little patch of sunshine. Come and help. You don't understand about fetching the ball, do you? Always leave it for me.

It's not in the shrubbery. Probably moles though. Arianna is good at digging to hunt for moles. Hasn't caught one yet but there's some big holes. No ball.

Bridget Arregger

Not under the table.

Not behind the shed.

Try the gravel again.

No.

Not in the long grass.

What about the short grass?

Ah! Getting closer.

I can't see it against the grass, but I can smell it here somewhere.

Here it is by the flowerpots.

Well done! Loki. You've found it.

I think she could see it all the time. She has that smile on her face. I toss it carelessly at her feet and it rolls under the bench where she is sitting. She looks at me. I get the ball and put it by her feet. It rolls a little, so I pick it up again and put it down gently. It touches her feet.

Well done, Loki. Thank You. Good boy.

I could do this all day and all night.

She can't see in the dark, but I can still smell the ball.

Getaway

The car door is opening.

'That was quick dear,' I say, 'I wasn't expecting you back so soon. Was the bank completely empty?'

That can't be right. I am not expecting her at all. I have left my wife. I left her this morning. It must be Harry getting into the driver's seat. I can't look up. I am busy trying to do up my fly. My wife, or was it Harry, conveniently left me an empty milk bottle knowing I would not last. Not a milk bottle. They don't make them anymore. One of those plastic things with a handle. A quart. It doesn't say it's a quart. They don't make those either. But I know it's a quart. I can't produce a quart. Don't need such a big bottle but my wife says it's easier for me to hold than the pint ones. I expect she's right.

I don't recognise the trouser legs next to me. Harry was wearing brown cords. These are black and shiny. Peter? Emily? Emily wears black shiny clothes. I look up.

'You must be Emily,' I start to say. But it's a man. I don't recognise him. Having a bad day. On a bad day, I can't recognise my wife. She reminds me. Sometimes, I think she's my Aunt Margaret.

'Who are you?' I say. He doesn't answer. He is holding a big bag and trying to squeeze it down on the floor between his legs. I try to take it from him. Plenty of room on my side.

'Gerroff,' he growls. He has managed to stash the bag. He is holding out his hand to me. I give him the milk bottle, although I haven't had time to put the lid on yet. My wife likes me to put the lid on before I give it to her. She tells me my pee stinks. That's why I have left her. Last week, was it? I wonder where Harry is.

The man is giving me back the bottle of pee. I take it and put the lid on. He is still holding out his hand. He is pointing to the ignition key slot. There is no key in it. I give him the bottle again and he throws it out of the window. He shouldn't do that.

'Who are you?' I ask.

'Never you mind,' he says. 'Gimme the keys.'

Harry left me the keys, I think, so I rummaged in my trouser cuff. Ah yes. I give the man the keys and he starts the engine.

'Where are we going?' I say.

'Never you mind,' he says. A man of few words. I like that. A refreshing change.

We are going dangerously fast. My wife doesn't drive that fast. Harry doesn't drive that fast. We're out in the countryside now.

Getaway

'Are we going for a drive in the country?' I ask the man.

He doesn't answer but he looks like my wife does when I've wet the bed. My trousers aren't a tiny bit wet. But he threw the bottle away. I may need that soon.

'I need a pee,' I say. I don't, but I don't like him driving so fast. I start to undo my fly. We screech to a halt.

'Get out,' he says.

'I can't,' I say. It's true. Harry has buckled me in with a padlock on the catch and put a special child lock thing on the front seat door. He doesn't want me to have an accident. He's a kind lad, Harry. Our first son, I think. Or is he a grandson?

The man is trying to undo my seat belt. He is using some very bad language. My wife would have a fit if she could hear him. I can hear police sirens. I wonder what they want.

Bridget Arregger

Blue Willow Trigger

His will?

Or my desire?

Or my good sense?

I cannot do this while driving.

Blue Willow takes my arms then my whole body into limpness.

I wallow, delta-waved. Washed in brain rhythms.

Every sound in the blind room, the distant street, fills my mind,

Until nothing and no-one matters.

Two minutes precisely and I surface to curious eyes.

Following a demonstration

and participation in learning self-hypnosis.

The Sky's the Limit

'Today, I'd like you to do a timeline of your life up to the present – place of birth, schools, house moves, jobs, family, that sort of thing. Anything that comes to mind. The dates don't have to be accurate...'

Sally groaned 'Not again!' and the therapist, yet another locum substitute, stopped speaking.

'Sorry, have you done this before?'

'Many, many times,' Sally said. 'You must be the fourth substitute since we started, with everyone off with Covid or whatever. They all start with this. Don't you read the notes?'

'Oh, sorry, but ...'

'Don't apologise,' Sally said. 'That's what you're supposed to say to me, isn't it? "Never apologise, never explain. Do what you wanna do." That's what they all say. Are my previous timelines in the notes?'

The therapist fumbled through the sheaf of papers in Sally's file.

'No, sorry.' She grinned, 'Oops, sorry.'

'So, what comes next?' Sally asked, graciously ignoring the apologies. 'Is there a next step?'

'There is, but you may have done this too, I'm afraid.'

'Well?'

'You continue the timeline with what you expect to happen in the next few years.'

'Right. Yes, done that. What next?'

'We talk through your expectations and see how realistic they are.'

'Right, done that. Next?'

'The sky's the limit'

'OK. Sounds new. Fire away!'

'If you could have anything you wanted, what would it be?'

'Ah, not new. Pity! Tried that. I dunno, do I? Never had anything much. Don't know what to say.'

'Do you do the lottery?'

'Nope.'

'Horses?'

'Nope, don't bet. Stupid waste of money.'

The Sky's the Limit

'OK. Do you dream of winning? finding millions?'

'Nah. Never bother with dreaming. Wouldn't help, would it? Frustrating.'

'OK. Let's go off-piste here.'

'Off-piste, is it? Ski, do you?

'No, I've never been skiing. Can't afford to ski. It's an expression. Let's try something different. Let's stop talking.'

'Not talking is different. Not talking would be nice.'

'How about we both take off our shoes and sit on the floor?'

'Sitting on the floor is different. OK.'

The therapist takes off her shoes and fetches a dusty cardboard box from behind a stack in the corner. It hasn't been moved for a while. She opens it and takes out coloured paper and crayons. Sally watches while she takes off her own shoes. She sniffs at them. Not too smelly.

'I haven't had the chance to do this here, too busy filling in forms, but my next few appointments have been cancelled, so we have time.'

'Now that really is different,' Sally says.

'I hope so,' the therapist says. 'Now, we're going to sit on the floor and close our eyes and I'll tell you a story. Maybe we'll draw something from the story afterwards and see where it takes us.'

'I can't draw,' Sally says.

'Doesn't matter. Neither can I.'

'The sky's the limit?' Sally says.

'Just so,' the therapist replies.

Prompt: The sky's the limit.

How I Met John

John and I met at Music Camp. It was August 1994 and it had been a disappointingly wet start to the ten days of camping. The youngsters were bored and restless and the organisers decided to have a competition for the Best Equipped Camper to give all 150 campers a task to take their minds off the rain. With the rotten weather I guessed most people would be putting together as much as they could possibly carry: rain hats, wellies, anoraks, buckets, mops, and a brolly although it was far too windy, in addition to the basics of tent, pegs, mallet, sleeping bag, air bed and pump, bed socks, hot water bottle…. It was cold at night even when it wasn't wet. On the appointed day, the rain stopped.

I was relatively new to camp and didn't know anyone well but was friendly with a few singers and had asked them to support me if I entered. They promised to cheer me on.

I decided to go for the three most important things I could think of and wrote three short verses, all beginning with 'As a Girl Guide, I was encouraged to Be Prepared' and 'As a scientist, I have been taught Least is Best.' I have lost the scrap of paper with the verses and don't remember them. But the gist of it was this.

'You need only three things to be a properly equipped music camper,' I said.

'First and foremost is a pencil to mark up your music, without which you are frowned on by the conductors.' To make sure I never forgot my pencil, I kept two or three stubs together with an eraser and pencil sharpener in a little plastic container on a lanyard around my neck. People often asked me what I kept in there. I opened the container and showed them one of my tiny pencils.

'Next thing you need is too big for my container, but I have it in my pocket.' And I produced a corkscrew. 'So long as you have one of these, you will find people invite you into their group and share their wine with you. You will not need to provide the wine and you will easily make friends.' There was a dire shortage of corkscrews in those days and no screw caps.

'The third thing you need,' I said, 'and this will answer all your questions about what I keep in here, is a few of these' - at which point I pulled out a small foil packet. 'With these, you will not need … your own tent … or sleeping bag… or bed socks or hot water bottle…or anything else much.'

Lots of laughter.

When all the competitors had had their go, the judges (two conductors and one of the cooks) started a minimalist repetitive chant 'We think, we think that we, we think,' and so on and declared I was the winner and had won first place to go up in the tethered hot air balloon.

How I Met John

The balloon had been tethered all morning to two trees and two trucks. It had been lifting the trucks partly off the ground. A few strong people hauled the balloon back to the ground and held it steady. It was exciting to be invited to climb aboard. A small crowd gathered to cheer and gradually, a queue formed. With several of us on board, we rose above the trees and had a magnificent view of the surrounding countryside. My trip was over much too quickly.

John was OO (orderly officer in charge of routine chores for the day) and asserted his 'right' to have a dance with the winner in the evening. When he put his arm around my shoulders for the Gay Gordons, I knew he was someone special.

Prompt: Every story starts somewhere.

Bridget Arregger

Your Beard

Morning, John, you're up early. Sorry, I didn't mean to make you jump; have you cut yourself? I'll find the TCP. I can see you do not like shaving in seawater. Our freshwater tanks are getting low, are they? How far are we from the next port? Three days if we're lucky? We do need to conserve then, so I'd better cook the veggies in half seawater from now on. Why don't you wait until we're at the marina for shaving? Better still, why not grow a beard?

What is your face like with a beard? You've never grown one? That will never do, and I like beards and I think it would suit you. I think you should grow a beard, starting now.

How do I know you don't like shaving in seawater? The salt stings, doesn't it? You flinched every time you put the blade to your chin and not because I made you jump. It has to be cold water, doesn't it? Hot salty water would be worse, and it would probably rust your razor and the saucepan, and we're running out of propane.

I can't say I like washing in seawater. Best to jump in the sea and forget about soap or shampoo. Wash the sand, sweat and old suntan lotion off by swimming round the boat a couple of times. It's too dark for that yet, I suppose.

But you'll soon be asking me to dive in and untie us from the palm tree when you're ready to set off. Five in the morning is the

Your Beard

best time for swimming while the water is warmer than the air and it is a pleasure to sink into the black water and head for the beach. Things to watch out for in the dark are jellyfish and those tiny stinging water ants that attacked Charlotte last time we were here.

Remember when Janice and I washed your shirts in seawater? You had been using the expensive suntan lotion marketed by the cancer-concern organisation, and where it had smeared onto the cotton, it converted to bright orange in the salt. Impossible to wash out later. We could write and complain but it is hardly a common occurrence for anyone to be washing their clothes in seawater and you can't expect them to test for every eventuality.

When do you think we'll be able to install the water maker? Reverse osmosis, did you call it? I know about osmosis and the way small molecules can pass through a membrane, but you'll have to explain how it takes the salt out. It would be good to have a constant supply of fresh water while we're sailing for weeks on end away from civilisation.

So, how's your beard coming along? Let me stand back and have a good look; now we're not fighting the wind. It does suit you. Quite the seasoned skipper with white hair and beard and nut-brown skin. It's better now you're past the scratchy stage, and you don't give me stubble burn every time we kiss. I love the soft silky feel of your beard.

Bridget Arregger

Prompt: write in the second person.

The Birds

Love in the time of COVID: Marianne

The bird cage could not protect her. Marianne Varga fastened open the aviary doors with garden wire and shivered in anticipation. The birds would not try to escape in the dark, so it might take them a while to realise they were free. She watched a robin hopping around the feeders. It watched her unconcerned. She could not tell if it had noticed the door was open. By mid-morning, like Marianne, they would all be gone.

Before she married Malcolm, she had not figured out why the wealthy financier liked to keep wild birds caged. She accepted his argument that they were in an aviary as big as their natural territory and did not suffer in any way. Caging them meant he could observe them any time he wanted. He had cameras on all the nests, nest boxes and strategically placed feeding stations. He could care for them. Every time there was a bird flu or other virus scare, he checked them all scrupulously and inoculated them if there was a vaccine available. They had a good life, he said, better than if they were wild.

She rubbed the bruises on her arms as she reached into her apron pocket and checked the baby alarm. Faintly through the crackle, she heard the unmistakable sound of his car. She shivered again as she stepped back out into the moonlight and then walked across the garden to the house.

The full moon hung huge and red. Like a harvest moon, Marianne thought, though it was early March. The low light illuminated every damp branch and they seemed to glow. Black lace shadows decorated the lawn. It struck her, then, how sharp moon shadows were. Each branch and tiny twig of the bare trees showed up crisp and black on the thin powdering of snow. More late snow was promised but it would not matter if her footprints remained. He would not be able to find her. Her bag was packed – supplies for Molly, nothing more.

Perhaps tonight, he would pause at the sight of the table set romantically for two. She had arranged candles and flowers. The red wine was already opened. She had chosen his favourite meal of chips and steak, cooked to his standard of over-done perfection. She had created something tastier for herself, as she often did, but pleasing him was the best route to a (relatively) quiet life.

However, he ignored her preparations. He ignored her altogether apart from an abrupt grunt as he pushed past her to go upstairs. He did not pester her but went straight to bed. She could hear him sneezing and complaining of itchy eyes and vague aches and pains. This gave her pleasure as she ate alone, savouring every mouthful before scraping the discarded steak and chips into the bin. Later, she crept in beside him, rubbing her own itchy eyes. She hugged her hot water bottle in preference to him. When she woke in the morning

The Birds

and found his dead body, stiff and cold in the bed beside her, it was a welcome shock.

Bridget Arregger

Clothes Maketh Women

Manners maketh the man but clothes maketh the woman?

What men *do* is important but how women *dress* is more important? What an upsetting gender split. I know this separation is widely assumed but I do not like such an artificial (one might say man-made) vision of the world.

However, I am aware what we wear is important for all people, men, women, trans, nonbinary, or other. It is significant for us and how we see ourselves and for other people and how they see us. And how we see others. Our clothes show what social groups we belong to and affect our mood and how we move and hold ourselves.

What do my clothes say about me? It is wonderful to dress up occasionally and choose clothes for the occasion. However, day to day, I like to be comfortable, clean, and dressed appropriately for any activity I am engaged in. Not being a fan of unregulated capitalism, I buy tops and coats in charity shops and sales; have several pairs of work trousers with lots of pockets, perfect for dog walking; cosy, sensible underpants; bras without wires; and socks and wide-toed, low-heeled shoes or boots from companies who cater for people who like to care for their feet. I wear a similar combination on most days, with changes appropriate to the weather or my mood. Most of my day-to-day clothes are lightly paint-splattered or mud-splattered, or both.

Clothes Maketh Women

Comfort and convenience are more important to me than appearance. I don't want to spend time choosing what to wear each day but can take the next clean one from the rail. What I do and what I am like is much more important to me than my appearance, most of the time. I don't much care how other people appraise me. I have chosen partners who share this view and have rejected anyone who judged otherwise.

Fortunately, I haven't worked anywhere with a strict dress code. In my first holiday job as a telephonist, I wore my normal student attire of flared turquoise trousers and orange jumpers, and no-one turned a hair. At least, no-one commented. I had not heard of dress codes in those days and was not aware lowly clerical staff in most jobs were expected to show up in white blouses and knee-length black, grey or navy skirts with stockings (in those days) and high heels. I was the sole person in that position; it was a newly-devised post, and I was working for electrical engineers, who were all men. I suspect they had not heard of dress codes either. Or didn't care.

When I started teaching science in a secondary school, I continued to wear trousers and covered my tops with a lab coat. Skirts would have been inconvenient when climbing up onto the benches or crawling about on the floor to demonstrate a tricky, thought-provoking concept. (You had to see it to believe it.) When I didn't have time to change out of my red motorcycle boots, I gained street cred. Some groups came to associate the red boots with an impromptu test and would be in fear of their manifestation. Then I took a job as an audio-visual technician at the local college. I was replacing a woman who had done clerical work, whereas I was happy to go into classrooms to set up the problematic reel-to-reel tape recorders and playback monitors. She had worn a regulation white blouse and navy skirt with heels, while I continued to wear a lab coat over polo neck jumpers and jeans, like the other (male) technicians. Gradually, I picked up part-time and then full-time science teaching in the college. I had no need to change my dress style.

But I do like to dress up from time to time. In my 40s, when I was between husbands, I did a lot of dating. I would dress in tight skirts with heels and flashy earrings for tea at the Savoy with BMW, Porsche, or Jaguar drivers or in cotton dresses or jeans for coffee with bikers in cafes by the river. When I was teaching a mixture of science, arts, and humanities, I occasionally dressed in a classic suit for the arts and flowing scarves for the science – to break the rules and confuse people. I don't think anybody noticed or cared.

I dated a transvestite for a while. He called himself a transvestite rather than a cross-dresser because he felt it described him more distinctly. Anybody could cross-dress for a party, he said, but he liked to dress up regularly and specifically for sex. He was not trying to be a woman. He liked the feel of the clothes. He had a selection of wigs a suitcase of make-up, and loved to dress in provocative

Clothes Maketh Women

women's dresses with lacy balconette bras, satin French knickers, and fishnet tights and encouraged me to do the same.

He was a photographer, and he took a series of photos of me in different styles of makeup and wigs. It was fun and he helped me learn a lot about myself.

One day, he made me up in heavy foundation, false eyelashes and bold, bright red lipstick with a shoulder-length auburn wig. By then I was teaching health psychology to nurses and the topic for the morning was altered body image. Nurses need to know how patients might feel when their appearance is altered by, say, an accident, or burns or surgery. That morning, I was scheduled to teach in one of the hospitals. The car park attendant who normally waved me past was reluctant to let me in as he did not recognise me. I had to show some ID.

I was early for the first class and set up the monitor, ready for a short video and handed out notes for the seminar. The nurses sauntered in, in twos and threes, and settled down, not taking any notice of me at all, not even to say good morning. I then faced the group, all experienced nurses, and said good morning to them. There was a sudden silence and then a burst of laughter. They had not recognised me, but they knew my voice. It led to some wonderfully lively discussion.

In the afternoon, I attended the college and knocked on the door of a close colleague. I knew I looked invitingly tarty and flamboyant and unrecognisable, even though I was wearing my own clothes. 'Hi,' I said, 'thanks for a wonderful evening.' My friend looked up startled. 'Do I know you?' he said. Another friend in the next room heard my voice and came in to say hello. Roars of laughter and applause. I went down to the canteen with the two of them and attracted a great many stares. Subsequently, people seeing the photos have said, 'She looks like a fun person to know.' Wasn't I always?

I am reminded of seeing a school play at a boys' junior school many years ago. Inevitably boys had to dress up as girls and it was remarkable how differently they moved, how they walked and how they sat down, preening themselves, when wearing a dress. Actors who wear Edwardian dresses say they feel quite different in those clothes compared with modern dresses. And I know I moved quite differently when heavily made up and with a wig, despite wearing my own clothes. Apparently, I smoothed down my skirt from time to time in a sexy way, although I was not conscious of doing it and, I am assured, did not normally do that.

I haven't worn a long dress for many years, but I used to walk in a particular way when dressed for ballroom dancing, which I loved. I'm not sure how I would feel if the opportunity arose now. I would be wobbly in heels.

Clothes Maketh Women

There is no doubt that what we wear affects how we feel. There is something special about silk underwear, smooth sheer tights, and heels. But this is not true of women alone. I have lost track of the number of men I have met who enjoy wearing silky underwear and stockings under their jeans. Some men, as well as women, like to relax in a kaftan when not at work. They simply like the feel.

There is something positive and active for women about wearing trousers. We can climb or stride or sit in a relaxed way without worrying if our knees are pressed together, and that has nothing to do with wanting to be men. Enjoying certain clothes need not have anything to do with cross-dressing.

Despite strong cultural influences, many male, female, trans, and nonbinary people can now wear the clothes they feel most comfortable in, at least at home and with close friends even if this is not yet acceptable at their place of work or in some public places.

I do wonder how the world would be if everyone felt free to wear any type of clothes they liked, regardless of whether their culture traditionally labels some garments as suitable for men and others as proper for women.

Prompt: Clothes maketh women

Bridget Arregger

Alter-ego

Loretta was Carol's alter-ego with her long red hair, tight skirts, and fuck-me shoes.

Tonight, Loretta was fidgety. She was tired of Carol's dowdy, risk-averse attitude to life. Loretta wanted action. It was New Year's Eve, and she was on the prowl. She, as Carol, had been invited to the office party and, as Loretta, had accepted.

She had to make do with Carol's boring office skirt and blouse (the skimpy tight skirts were all in the imagination), but she knew it was posture, way of walking and mannerisms that made the difference. So, she imagined a new little black number and sling-backs and sauntered into the crowded room, crossing her feet so her buttocks rocked like a catwalk model. A few heads turned.

Better not overdo it, Carol over-ruled Loretta. She walked more gracefully, allowing her hips to sway gently.

'What will you have to drink, Carol,' someone offered. 'There's a good punch.'

Carol was astonished anyone wanted to speak to her. She smiled in delight.

'Yes, p-punch, p-please,' she stammered, 'that would be g-great.'

Alter-ego

Loretta reasserted herself. She smiled more widely. 'That would be great,' she repeated, without stammering, and accepted a filled paper cup.

The punch was delicious.

'Who made this?' She said in genuine surprise.

'I did,' came the reply, with a wicked grin. 'Better not have too much if you're not used to it.'

Loretta and Carol both wavered. Loretta was bold but not foolish. How much punch would give her a good time without making an idiot of herself?

She looked at the punch-conjurer. He grinned again.

'Drink up,' he said. 'It's not lethal.' He had a mischievous face, not good looking in any conventional sense but with enormous appeal.

Carol sipped her drink slowly, not knowing what else to say, and then Loretta finished it in one gulp and proffered the empty cup to the mischievous face. She did not know his name, did not recognise him. She must have looked puzzled.

'I'm Jim,' he said, 'you probably don't know me, but I come past your desk most days. I'm glad you've come tonight. I've never known how to say hello. Most days,' he hesitated, '...most days you don't look up when I come past, but you have a sparkle about you, and I've wondered…'

'Please give me some more of your delicious punch,' Carol and Loretta answered in unison. The chimes are about to begin.'

Together, they drank a toast to the New Year.

Prompt: starting something new.

Her Decision

What a waste of time! No, not a waste of her time exactly. It was important for her to be here. It was her decision. But people were so ineffective at taking part in committee meetings.

She couldn't decide which were worse, men or women. Businessmen inhabit a world made up of people and women. People make decisions, women don't. Such men can seem perfectly polite, appear to listen to what a woman has to say, and nod thank you, but somehow not give much credit to what was said.

Women were essential to business, there was no doubt about it, but in mindless things like making the tea, arranging the flowers, listening nicely, patting the men on the back or offering to do something useful like write memos, do the research, or paperwork, or laminate the notices. Women didn't contribute to important decisions. They weren't allowed to, but that was simply the natural order of things. It was the way the world worked.

Women, on the other hand, provided there were no men present, made decisions - eventually. They talked a great deal and really listened to each other, to the doubts, to the alternatives. Round and round they'd go. First, one suggestion would be a good idea, then someone would find a snag and it would be rejected, and another would seem best until it too was put aside. It was unlikely a decision would be made soon, but lots of ideas would be floated, no conclusion drawn, no one selected to carry it through, and it would be shelved until next time.

Men talked as much. Each loved the sound of his own voice and would drone on and on. But the decision would have been made by a small minority beforehand, on the golf course or the squash court, where few women venture except in their roles as girlfriends or wives, and when everyone's minds had drifted elsewhere, the magic words of 'that's agreed then' would be voiced and no one would be quick enough to raise any objections before a signature was appended and the paper given to a woman to put through the system.

So why was she here? She was an instigator, a facilitator, a catalyst who helped others formulate their ideas and produce a comprehensive and comprehensible proposal. She sounded out *everyone*'s views in advance, weighed the advantages and disadvantages, and laid out the arguments. When she knew everyone's opinions and could predict the likely outcome, she would convene a brief meeting for final comments and decisions.

That was when she was paid to do her job. Now, retired, invited to work with a bunch of retired enthusiasts to help the charity become more efficient, she sat back while men spouted (endlessly) and women found fault (endlessly) until, in the fullness of time, something would be achieved. It would take time to help them learn. Her decision.

Prompt: what a waste of time.

Moving on

Right, let's get this meeting finished as soon as possible.

Matters arising?

Nothing that isn't in the main agenda? OK.

Item 3. Plans for putting in a disabled toilet. How's that going?

Yes, Sheila?

The project manager is going slow? How come?

He's on holiday? That's not good timing for us with prices rising all the time.

He's having an affair with the boss's wife?

Let's not go there. Moving on.

Item 4. Who's handling that?

Prompt: Moving On, in any interpretation.

Bridget Arregger

March or Dance? The Changing Use of Rhythm in Poetry.

March: walk in a military manner with a regular measured tread. Google's English dictionary accessed March 2024.

Dance: the movement of the body in a rhythmic way, usually to music and within a given space, for the purpose of expressing an idea or emotion, releasing energy, or simply taking delight in the movement itself. From an article in www.britannica.com with reference to the painting Peasant Dance by Pieter Bruegel the Elder c1567 accessed March 2024.

Rosie put aside her notebook. It would be difficult to march in a wild undignified manner, she mused, but John Cleese managed it in his Ministry of Silly Walks. She visualised serried ranks of John Cleese clones. Marching.

Dancing was something else.

She selected Stravinsky's Rite of Spring on her playlist, to be followed by Ravel's Bolero and her favourite YouTube clips of contemporary expressive dance and began to move. Her OU dissertation would have to wait.

Prompt: March (in any interpretation).

What's in Your Pockets?

'What's your name?'

'Mmm mm mmmmmmm mm'

'Your groans have the rhythm of speech patterns.'

Who is he, I wonder. Don't know and he can't tell me as he is bound and gagged, writhing in the mud.

How did he get there? Don't know yet, I was writing another story in my head, and he appeared. Sound of horses' hooves. Someone coming? No the sound is fading, his assailant perhaps.

'What's in your pockets?'

'May I?'

'Mm mm mmmm.'

Unused, blue, heavy paper table napkin embossed with restaurant logo, red silk handkerchief, retractable steel tape measure, eraser, dyed purple feather, grit and mud, a pencil stub, mouldy apple core. No money, no ID.

So, He likes strong colours? He lives with someone who likes strong colours? Someone who dances? He often needs to measure things. Conjurer's assistant? He's a conjurer? Failed Houdini?

His assailant connived with his wife for the trick to go wrong and they have dumped him out here while they elope? Can't elope with a married person. Not wife. Daughter perhaps. Or his assistant was lover.

Why was he deceived by his wife/lover? – he should have been able to see through her. He is skilful with deception: perpetrating *and* detecting.

Must be daughter. Why has he been preventing her attachment?

Uh oh, baby crying. In my head? His daughter had a baby? Is pregnant?

No! Not in my head. Real baby crying. Mine.

Must go.

'Sorry mate, hope someone comes to untie you soon.'

'Mmm mm mmmmmm.'

Prompted by the suggestion that if you want to know more about your characters, you need to examine what they have in their pockets.

Serendipity

Serendipity

Good. Bessie critically surveyed the eight back packs, set down from habit in a row on the waiting room bench.

She picked them up again, one at a time, and dropped them randomly on the floor. Who'd have thought it? Two sets of twins, now fourteen and twelve years old, then triplets, eight years old. All girls, non-identical, all different shapes and sizes and colours like the new back packs.

Gone were the carefully matched bags with the same identifying ribbon that would have looked apposite if arranged in order of size on the bench. Gone too were the girls' seven sets of plaits, with identifying ribbons, and matching outfits.

The waiting room was empty except for herself; the girls having gone in search of ice creams. It was a hot day. Someone had spent some effort decorating the room with posters advertising holidays in exotic places like Bali, St Lucia and Sri Lanka. They had been to all these and more. They had been good holidays. Tony had organised them down to the last detail - all booked in advance, all activities prescribed. Yes, they had been good.

Good. Expertly planned. Nothing to surprise.

Tony, sadly, was no more. They had mourned. They had missed the order and the predictability.

Then, to their surprise, they felt free.

They would have a different kind of holiday.

They would take a train, each carrying a change of clothes and a few items of personal value. When they felt they'd had their money's worth and saw somewhere enticing, they'd disembark.

They wouldn't need consensus. One person shouting 'yes!' would be enough. They were good at taking turns.

They would find a youth hostel, hire a camper or a boat, or take a bus or another train, as the fancy took them. A new place whenever they wanted.

Bessie had a vague plan to be back in time for school. They had the whole summer holiday: six weeks of freedom, ripe for serendipity.

Prompt: serendipity.

Grief and Laughter

Mary shivers in the cold early morning air as she sets out cautiously to explore the countryside around her new home. She follows a woodland path leading to the lake. There is a light mist everywhere and distant trees fade into the hills beyond. Around her, the insubstantial wood seems shrouded in shadow that threatens to intensify her sadness.

The path twists and turns as it drops downwards. The vegetation becomes more densely packed, the shadows increase, and she loses sight of the lake. In the gloom, her eyes burn as tears begin to form.

The path emerges at the lakeside and stops at an old half-submerged wooden jetty. She pauses, fearful, unable to venture further, and through her tears tries to take in more details of this deserted spot. Reflections of trees on the opposite bank blend into the water. Broken reeds near her hands hang limply as if bowed down by sorrow more intense than her own.

Swamped with grief she imagines walking out onto the rotten wood and sinking slowly into the deep cold water. As she takes a hesitant step onto the planking it moves under her feet.

The mist intensifies and obscures everything. Sounds become muffled. There is nothing to cling to. The rickety wood shifts repeatedly under her weight. She sways and staggers, slow to regain her balance, bewildered by the absence of sensory connection with the earth. Darkness invades her. It should be easy now to step out into nothingness, but she remains still, petrified. Time ceases.

She catches a whiff of wood smoke. Gradually, small sounds penetrate the fog of her consciousness: a slight splash of water, the cry of a moorhen, and the distant hum of a motor. She hears faint echoes of childish laughter. Two figures appear at the end of the jetty, materialising out of the swirls of mist. They look like two pixies with pointed hats and thin legs. Mary takes a step in their direction, but they dissolve back into the haze.

She retreats onto the solid path and watches as the sun rises and the mist evaporates. She gazes at the tranquil scene and ponders how to paint it, realising as she does so that her misery has vanished with the pixies. Warmth creeps back into her limbs. She finds crocuses at her feet. There are new leaf buds on the trees. She must grieve but it need not overwhelm her another time. She will start her new life in this wonderful place full of magic and mystery, never far from the laughter of children.

Prompt: a photo of a jetty at the side of a lake, with two indistinct figures.

One Year Older

Janet woke with a start. It was 7:15 but she didn't need to look at the clock to know what had woken her. There was unaccustomed silence. Silence and the absence of certain distinctive familiar smells.

She usually woke at 7:15 but there wasn't any need anymore. She could stay in bed as long as she liked. She wondered how long it would take before she could relax and enjoy a little more time in bed. No need to go for a bracing walk before breakfast. No need to mop the kitchen floor.

Janet wasn't sure how she'd adapt to living completely on her own. She was a natural early riser, but it would feel strange not to have a regular daily commitment. Being a creature of habit, she had regular wash days and other household chores best done first thing in the morning. Her routine hadn't changed since her mother's daily schedule and *her* mother's before that. Monday washday. Tuesday or Wednesday ironing, depending on how dry the clothes were. Thursday, baking for the weekend. Shopping every day in the market before breakfast to buy fresh bread and the best produce. Now, there was no need. There wouldn't be much washing or ironing. She could use shops nearer than the market. She could shop once a week. She could shop late in the evening when the prices were reduced. There was no-one to mind whether the peas were fresh or frozen. No-one to require heavy items like potatoes or tinned food. Her previously demanding, caring life was suddenly ended.

The last few years had seen everyone off: her father, her grandmother, her mother, her husband. (She had no siblings, no children.) And now, Benny.

Poor Benny. Like the others, he'd been incontinent for his last few months. Poor Benny had barked as regularly as clockwork at 7:15 every morning for all of his long life, with a day or two of adjustment each time the clocks changed. Until the last months, this had signified a joyful greeting of each new day and the need to go out in the garden. This had given Janet some joy too. But recently it had become a bark and whine of apparent shame as he stood at the garden door with head hanging low and his tail between his legs. She had continued to care for him, like the others, lovingly, unconditionally. It would have been his birthday today, but he didn't quite make it. She had bought him a new collar with lights for the dark evenings. It was still wrapped, and it was not too late to return it. It was her birthday too. Another year on but no-one to share the day.

Janet swung her legs out of bed. It wasn't Thursday, but she could bake a cake. She could pop into the library. She could …

Prompt: one year older

Great Aunt Zilla

'Don't you think my sister looks lovely, Aunty Zilla?' Twelve-year-old Susan sat down by her great aunt.

'Harrumph,' Great Aunt Zilla blew down her nose and coughed, 'those silly shoes, and all that make up and her dress isn't ironed.'

'That's the fashion, Aunty Zilla; it's crushed silk like Princess Di and expensive.'

'Harrumph, too much money. What is she thinking of? Marrying into *that* family?'

'She's not marrying into the family, Aunty Zilla. That's not how it works these days. They love each other.'

'I hope so, dear, but that's not what counts is it?'

'What do you mean? *Love is all you need.*' Susan sang the refrain.

'Yes, we sang that back in my young days too. It was new then and we truly thought we were right.'

'But they've known each other for ages. They know they're in love.'

'In love, dear? Probably, but they don't know each other. I lived with my first husband for two years before getting married . . .'

'You did? Susan was startled and could see she needed to think of her ancient aunt in a new way.

'Yes, it wasn't quite the done thing then, but we thought it was a good idea. Not marrying for lust but waiting until we were sure. But how could we be sure?'

'But why not? What didn't you know after two years? That's a long time.'

'It's a short time but we knew the little things.'

'Such as?'

'You know, dear, how he squeezed the toothpaste tube clumsily in the middle and I liked to keep it tidy.'

Susan laughed. 'Easy to solve. A tube each.'

'Yes, we did that, dear, and if we'd had the money, we'd have had a bathroom each. Preferably a bedroom each. Ideally a house each. Visit from time to time.'

'Aunty, don't be silly.'

'I'm not being silly. A house each. With a housekeeper each.'

'Which one would the children live in?'

Great Aunt Zilla

'Ah, children. That's where it all began to go wrong. When you want to marry, Susan, dear, make sure you choose a man who's good with children.'

'I don't want to get married, Aunty Zilla. I don't do boys.'

Great Aunt Zilla laughed heartily. 'You don't, eh? In my young days it was the boys who did the girls. I met my first boyfriend when I was sixteen. No need to raise your eyebrows young lady; sweet sixteen and never been kissed was the norm. My first boyfriend was an old and sophisticated twenty. He asked me if I would like him to 'do' me. Somehow, I knew vaguely what he meant although we didn't talk much about such things in those days. I considered his surname and decided it wouldn't go with my first name so he couldn't be the one for me and I said no. Civilly of course. So, he did my sister instead, once, and I don't think either of us saw him again.'

'What was his name?'

'Miller. Simon Miller.'

So, if you'd married you would have been ...'

'Zilla Miller. I didn't fancy that.'

Prompt: The bride's great aunt.

Bridget Arregger

Haunted

I saw my sister again yesterday. I could make her out ahead of me in the crowd as I pushed my way down Oxford Street. The determined way she walked. That toss of her head. That shake of the greying curls. No mistaking her. No chance of catching her up. Then she was gone. I see her frequently, a glimpse, a reflection in a shop window, perhaps, or getting onto a bus, always out of reach. She does not see me. She is not looking for me. Why would she? How can she know I am here? Such a horrible death.

Prompt: Ghosts. The surviving sister imagining she is seeing her sister, glimpsing her ghost? Or is the spirit watching the surviving one?

My Name is Sandra

Sandra's tales of small-ad, casual and online dating in middle age: Chapter One

My name is Sandra. Not my real name of course but when you start to talk about sex, people like to talk about you. It gets difficult going to the supermarket. People stare and point. Women stick pins into little voodoo dolls and men come to the house to offer to do those manly jobs that women can't do and casually drop into the conversation that their wives don't understand them.

Living alone, I am grateful for help with certain jobs that require brute strength, skills I have not acquired, or two pairs of hands, but my moral code does not embrace married men. I allow myself to embrace married men but that's all. No sex. I don't think it's wrong if it doesn't hurt anyone, but it's too complicated. I hear too often that men promise to leave their wives but can't, or women come to demand that they do so, and there is never a happy ending.

All relationships reach a testing plateau, don't they? It requires a secure friendship and companionship to outlast the sexual fervour. And my memory is not good. In a senior moment, I may give something away – and hurt someone.

When my husband left me for another woman, I had straggly, mousy hair rapidly going grey and was wearing shapeless, colourless clothes. Mousy clothes, mousy hair, mousy personality. What I saw in the mirror was unattractive. Perhaps my husband was justified in leaving me. On the other hand, I had never liked making love with him after the first thrill faded as it became more and more like struggling with a sack of potatoes, leaving me hot, tired and unsatisfied.

I could have faded into obscurity, living alone, nursing my sorrows. I was rescued by a private eye. The Private Eye. I started reading the small-ads in the back. Eye Love. Woman WLTM man WSOH etc.

I composed my first ad.

I had nothing to lose.

I had one date that was a pleasant enough evening.

I had chosen Private Eye so that we would have something to talk about – the cartoons, at least. However, he had never read Private Eye and had no idea what kind of magazine it was. He did not appear to know what satire was. He had a different kind of SOH, I imagine.

He was a printer and his mates had told him Private Eye was the best place to meet people. We did not share political views. We didn't like the same books, music, movies, activities…. He was due to go skiing the following week. Not an activity or holiday that I fancied much, even if I could afford it. Which I couldn't.

We had nothing in common and it wasn't going to lead anywhere but as we parted, he gave me a peck on the cheek, and he smelled nice. It was enough to make me realise things could get better.

Buoyant, I had a complete makeover. Ate more healthily. Fish, rice and vegetables. My skin and hair improved. I had my hair re-styled. I changed my job.

I'm a history graduate. Now metamorphosed into a librarian, not the usual type to be associated with having a good time. I look like the stereotype, I'm told. There are many stereotypes, I believe, from frumpy to forbidding.

I have adopted the academic style with cropped white hair, long bony nose with specs, high forehead, and modest clothes with neat collars. The right men know that under the prim exterior I will be up for it.

Subsequently, I have found the library is sufficient meeting place and I can quickly weed out the no-hopers, but when times are quiet, I try another ad or, of course, more recently, go online.

Some men ask outright; others enquire courteously with their eyebrows and a certain air visible across a large room or between the book stacks. I can choose to respond or ignore. If I respond with an equally coded eyebrow, things can move on swiftly.

If I ignore them, most men do not try again. Win some, lose some. They will go elsewhere.

There are a few who persist and may need a brief puzzled frown and, of course, there are those who have forgotten they tried last month and need several shrugs and frowns before they develop a memory. They're mostly harmless.

VHF Possibilities

Come in, Come in, Tin Tin

Tin Tin, Tin Tin, Tin Tack, Tin Tack

Tin Tin, Tin Tin, Tin Tack

Tin Tack, Tin Tack, Blue Tack

Blue Tack, Tin Tack, up one and hold?

hold

Get a Life, Get a Life, Lazybones

Lazybones, Get a Life, pick a channel,

Lazybones, Lazybones, Whalebones, Whalebones

Whalebones, Turtlebones

Anybody got a trombone?

Dear Bridget, Dear Bridget, UR My Darling, UR My Darling

UR My Darling, Dear Bridget, ... allons soixante neuf? Over.

Bridget Arregger

Peakes stand by on six nine. Over.

OK, go...

Bottoms Up, Bottoms Up, My Lady Love

Whatever, Whatever, Mischief

Follow Me, Follow Me, Easy Lady

Why not, Why not, Why not

Sweet Music, Wild Thing

Ooh..., go..., Sweet..., Wild..., ...Over, Whatever..., ...going up, Stand by..., ...going down...Darling, ...Hold, ...come back, Come in please, That's a roger, Ooh la la..., Again, ...and wait, Wherever, Whenever, However, Mm, Mm, Mood Indi..., Go, In, ...Out, In..., you're breaking up, come..., Ooh..., U2?

Sweet Music, Sweet Music, Wild Thing

Wild

Kiss Me Kate, Kiss Me Kate, this is Red Devil, Red Devil

Kiss Me Kate

VHF Possibilities

In Your Dreams, In Your Dreams, Shark

Farewell, Farewell,

Out.

This is a play on the names of yachts and VHF radio etiquette as heard on the daily yachtie radio net while sailing in the Caribbean. Names are usually repeated so that they can be heard when reception is poor.

Printed in Great Britain
by Amazon